D1584940

No stars
at the circus

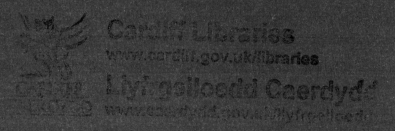

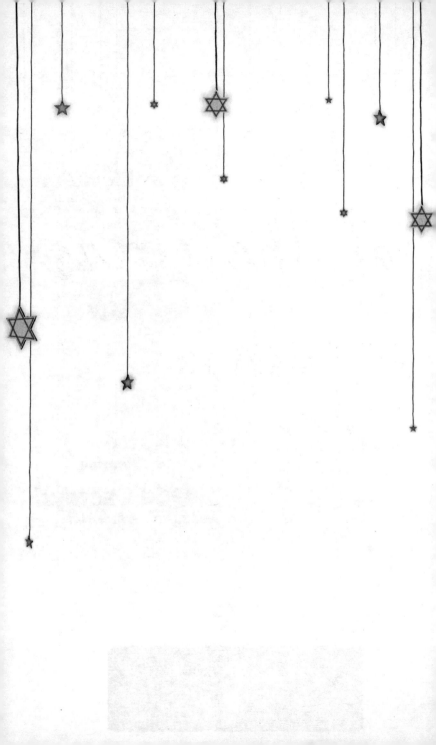

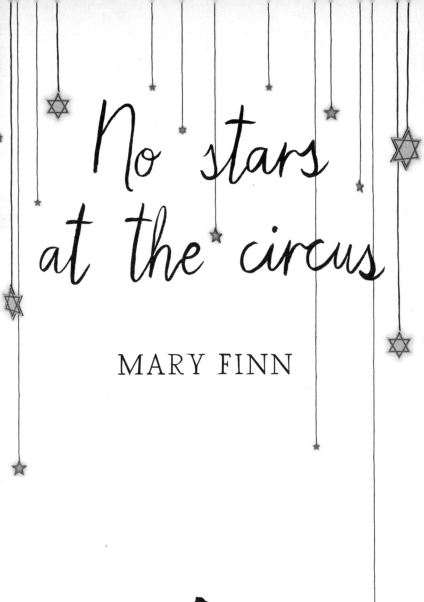

No stars
at the circus

MARY FINN

**WALKER
BOOKS**

First published in Great Britain 2014 by Walker Books Ltd
87 Vauxhall Walk, London SE11 5HJ

2 4 6 8 10 9 7 5 3 1

Text © 2014 by Mary Finn
Cover photographs 2014 © Laura Yurs / Gettyimages and
Berliner Verlag / Archiv / dpa / Corbis

This book has been typeset in Stempel Schneidler

Printed and bound in Great Britain by Clays Ltd, St Ives plc

British Library Cataloguing in Publication Data:
a catalogue record for this book is available from the British Library

ISBN 978-1-4063-4733-3

www.walker.co.uk

For John

MY WILL

This is the Last Will and Testament of Jonas Alber.

In the event of my death, my money goes to Mama. If you can't find her, it's to be kept for Nadia.

I leave all my clothes to La Giaconda for her son, Tommaso, who is my size, though he is younger than me. I leave my flea circus to Signor Corrado because he showed me how to train the fleas. I don't have any of the fleas here, in case the Professor gets upset about them, but I have all the carriages with me. They are made of real silver. Papa put proper hallmarks on them, so they are worth a fair bit.

If the key to my home at rue de la Harpe can be found and if our belongings are still there, I leave all my books to my friend Jean-Paul Lambert. He can have my roller skates too, which are under the bed, and my globe, which is on the windowsill. Those are the only things I have left, except for my comb. If Alfredo wants that he can have it.

Signed *Jonas Alber*, aged ten years.
23 August 1942

TO THE PERSON WHOSE JOB
IT IS TO READ WILLS

I wrote and signed my will at the Professor's house, 12 rue Cuvier, Paris 5, but my family's address is 10a rue des Lions, Paris 4. Before that we used to live at 31 rue de la Harpe, Paris 5, over my father's shop. That is where our piano is still but it belongs to my mother, not to me, so I cannot leave it to anybody.

Please check *everywhere* for *all* our belongings and keep them safe for my family. My papa wrote a will and testament when the war began, so look out for that too. I saw it once in his desk. That's how I knew the way to write mine.

I know that a testament is also a story. The rest of what I write will be that kind of testament. You can read it if you like but it's really for Mama, Papa and Nadia, wherever they are. It will explain what I've been doing since I last saw them.

That was nearly six weeks ago.

J.A.

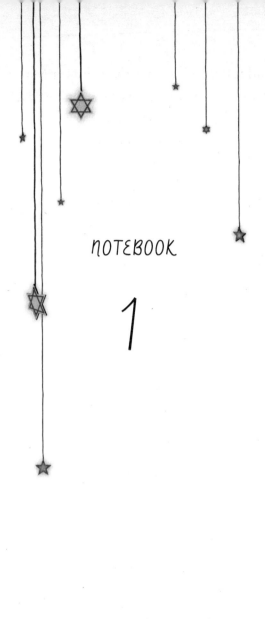

NOTEBOOK

1

WHY I HAVE WRITTEN A WILL

I am living in rue Cuvier now because Signor Corrado brought me to see the Professor yesterday. He fixed it up for me to come here and be safe. So far, I have been safe in this house for exactly one day.

The Professor was my mother's music teacher when she was young. Signor Corrado knew where to find him because of the card Mama gave me, with the Professor's name on it, and where he lived. So we came here early yesterday morning, on Papa's bike.

Signor Corrado knocked on the door of No. 12 quite loudly. He hadn't said a word since we'd crossed the bridge. I think he was nearly as scared as I was. But you wouldn't have known that from what he said when the thin old man opened the door. He held it wide open, not like most people do – leaving room for only half their face to look out. His was very bony.

"You are the professor of music, Monsieur?" Signor Corrado asked. "This man?" He showed him Mama's card. I swear he sounded every bit as rough as a policeman.

The old man nodded but he said nothing. So Signor Corrado lifted my arm up in the air as if I was a boxer who had won a match and said, "This is Jonas Alber, whose mama was once the Mademoiselle Anne Berlioz you will remember so well, of course. Can we come in?"

It was pretty rude to ask that straight out when you'd just met someone. Nobody lets strangers into their house now.

But the old Professor waved us inside, anyway. Even though you could see he was still blinking away at the sight of us. Even though Signor Corrado had an ordinary jacket and trousers on – nothing striped, no bows or rosettes.

When the door was closed and we were in the hall, Signor Corrado didn't waste any time. He just told the Professor it wasn't safe for me to stay with his family any longer.

"You know the reason as well as I do, Monsieur.

That rabble is working night and day to ferret out any poor souls they missed catching last month. They're scum. I'm not afraid to say that and I'm sure you're not afraid to hear it, being a cultured man."

The Professor opened his mouth but he said nothing. Again.

Signor Corrado pointed at my head. "Look at the boy's hair! Look at mine!"

He tried to comb his hair with his fingers but they got stuck in it, like they always did.

"What would *you* think, Monsieur, if you were one of *them*? Would you say we looked like family?"

We don't. I have fair straight hair and all the Corrados have black hair as thick as wire, so I don't even look like their second cousin ten times removed. So all these weeks, Signor Corrado had kept thinking the Germans would come one day and pounce on me and take me off to a jail, or somewhere. It's true they could have, because the fairground is open even when there's no show on. And everybody who works there knows everybody else. They know who belongs and who doesn't.

They know I don't.

But Signor Corrado didn't mind that. He has a great trust in the fairground people.

"Artists don't tell tales, Jonas," he told me. "Life

is too dodgy for us. We need one another. No, the real problem is other people. One of your old neighbours might pass through here one day and recognize you."

Well, no Jews were going to come to the fair any day soon, so that ruled out good old rue des Lions. And all our neighbours from before are too old, or they work too hard or else they have no money to come to the fair.

I told Signor Corrado that but he only wrinkled his nose. He said there were lots of people who might tell the Germans about me just to get some extra food coupons for their families.

But in the end it was no neighbour. It was Pimply Arms who gave me away. He hated Jews. That was when I had to leave the Corrados.

Anyway, Signor Corrado told the Professor all these things. He started off with what had happened on that day in July. The reason I was living with his family.

He said, "We just don't know where the boy's family was sent to. We became his second family. Now, Monsieur, I'm asking you to be his third."

I looked around while he was talking. The walls were painted the colour of red cabbage and there was a row of small pictures along one of them. The only one I could see properly showed a green wind-up bird on a shelf. Mama had told us about that picture!

At the end of the hall there was a long set of stairs going up and a short staircase going down. There were no names or numbers on any of the doors I could see and they had no locks. So did the Professor live here all on his own? With all these rooms to spare?

He must, because suddenly he said yes. Just yes. I knew that meant he was going to take me for a while but it also meant he didn't have to go into any of the rooms to ask anybody else if they thought it was a great idea to have Jonas Alber coming to live with them.

Just him and me then. In a huge house. What would that be like?

But he was staring at me.

"You look like your mother, Jonas," he said. "I remember her as if it was yesterday, the day she came to my door. She was so small for her age but she had such promise." He coughed and cleared his throat. "All right, you can stay here until we find somewhere better for you."

Signor Corrado shook hands with him. "You'll know where to find me, Monsieur," he said. "Everyone knows me at the fairground in Nation."

He pressed my head against his chest as if it was

a brand-new football he was testing. He kissed the top of it. Then he was out the door and gone. If he'd looked back through the letterbox for a joke he would have seen the Professor and me staring at the door. We must have looked like two dogs locked out in the rain, except we were locked in and Signor Corrado was the one outside.

But he didn't look. I suppose he just got back on Papa's bike and cycled home.

So here I am. And that's why I wrote my will on a separate page. It's in case the Germans storm in here and find me after all.

MY FRIENDS, THE CORRADOS

I was sorry to leave the Corrado family for three reasons:

No. 1 – Because they are very kind people.

No. 2 – Because I was able to show off my fleas and their tricks at the fair and earn some money. If I say so myself, my fleas were very well trained. And Signor Corrado said he had never seen anything as beautifully made as the carriages Papa made for my flea circus. He would lift them up and stroke them.

"Bellissima," he said every time. In Italian that means not just beautiful but *really* beautiful. The Corrados are Italian but they can speak pretty good French, even Tommaso, who doesn't say much in

any language unless it's about football.

Papa told me the carriages were in the style of Louis Quatorze, the Sun King. My sister Nadia said they look as if they had rolled straight out of a fairy tale. She said they were shrunk by a spell and one day it will wear off and we will have real silver carriages to ride in. She's always thinking mad things like that.

When we were sick together in the same room I let Nadia use the carriages in her puppet theatre. But not with the fleas, of course. They stayed in their box.

The box with the carriages is now in my coat pocket. Which is now in the trunk under the window. Which I'm not allowed to look out of, even though this room is right up at the top of this huge house.

But who'd see me? There's a big canvas curtain right across the window. I could peep out. *No problemo*. That's what Tommaso used to say when he was kicking a goal from a corner.

I bet you can see lots from up here. This used to be a maid's room in the old days, the Professor said, long before he bought the house. Poor old maid. Maybe she had the best view in Paris but there are no wardrobes or dressers in the room, just the skinny old bed and the trunk.

And everything that belongs to me has to go into the trunk.

"Just in case," the Professor said.

In case what? I wanted to say. In case the Germans track me down?

I suppose I'm to get into the trunk as well, if he can't stop the Germans from rushing upstairs. Because none of them would be smart enough to guess there was a boy in the trunk.

Ha ha.

He didn't say that, of course. He said I had to be completely quiet all the time even though the walls of the house are so thick. Nobody must know I'm here, he said, not even a mouse.

"But there are no mice. I'm pretty sure of that, Jonas."

That was supposed to be a joke because he smiled. So I smiled too.

At least the window looks out onto the street. Even if I'm not allowed to look out of it I know that much. I can hear street sounds – carts going by, people shouting, that kind of thing.

The thing about the trunk is all a bit daft anyway because he brought things up for me and he said they needn't go into it. He gave me a grammar work book, some ordinary pencils and a long thin propelling pencil that has a tiny hot air balloon going up and down inside the glass. He told me one of his students left it behind last year. He also brought up a mathematics book, a mythology book and two encyclopedias. One is A–L, the other is M–Z. He says he has books about the lives of the great composers too, if I would like to read them.

There's a piano downstairs in this house. I saw a bit of the keyboard through a door when we came up here yesterday. I'd love to play it but guess what, I'll never be able to because he's afraid to let me come down from this pokey room at the top of the house.

He says that's because he has no papers for me. But nobody has, except Mama and Papa. Not even Signor Corrado had my papers. Unfortunately, that was what made him even more worried about me.

"If you don't have papers you're *finito*, Jonas," he said.

It *is* a big problem. I don't blame anyone for being afraid.

Maybe the Professor will get braver later on. If I do everything he asks it might encourage him. He is a little like one of those long thin caterpillars that stand up on their back legs and wave their heads at you but are squishy if you stand on them by mistake.

Maybe he just doesn't like having a boy in his

house. Maybe it's nothing to do with me not having papers.

Anyway, the good news is that I have four big notebooks from the Deyrolle shop to write in. Signor Corrado gave me the set as a present. Three of them are in the trunk. One is on my lap but it's going under the mattress when I'm finished writing this. My will is folded inside the beginning pages.

When I was with the Corrados in their yellow van I used to sleep on cushions under Alfredo's bunk. Madame Fifi's bed was behind a curtain but even so I could hear her poodles every night. I never knew dogs could snore like that. I suppose they sounded so loud because I was on the floor and so were they. They had fleas too but they were not trained like mine were. They were stupid dog fleas!!!!

I made notches under Alfredo's bed to mark how long it was since I'd seen my family. There were five when I left, one for every week. Now I have scraped five new notches on one of the legs of this bed, where the Professor will not see them. Two days from now I will make the sixth.

I almost forgot! The third reason I was sorry to leave the Corrado family: they were lots of fun to be around.

HOW TO WRITE A STORY

Monsieur Lemoine, the French teacher in my old school, told us that when we write a story we should start at the beginning, continue as far as the middle and then get to the finishing tape without losing our shorts or our shoes. He said it's not as easy as it sounds.

I probably won't have Monsieur Lemoine again for class because I will be going to the collège next and he will stay behind. He likes me. He says I have a spirit of adventure that would serve a pirate well.

But he ruined that when he said, "Of course, very few teachers will appreciate this quality of yours, Jonas. Especially if you are late for school because of your nefarious activities."

He wrote down "nefarious" in my copybook. It means "bad", but what he was talking about was the school day he saw me in the Luxembourg Gardens when I was helping to set out the chairs for the puppet show. Stéphane, who owns the puppets, used to let me watch for free if I did that for him.

But that was in the old days, when we lived in rue de la Harpe. When I went to school.

SO HERE IS
THE BEGINNING!

I won't start with the war, or with the Germans sneaking into France, because everybody in the whole world knows about those things. Anyway, I was much younger then. I didn't know so much about what was going on. I remember the gas masks Nadia and I had and how Mama got so cross when we played with them, especially if Jean-Paul was there too. Which he was a lot because he was my best friend. He liked to come to our place because he had no brothers or sisters.

"Gas masks are not toys, they're meant to save your life," Mama shouted at us. "And Jean-Paul has his own at home to play with if he wants to."

We pretended we were giant insects because the

masks had big buggy eyes. But when you breathed in with the mask on, it made a noise like a cave monster, not an insect.

Then the summer came and nearly everyone in Paris ran away because the Germans were coming. Even Jean-Paul's family packed up and left. We didn't. Papa said he wouldn't leave our shop to be looted by Germans. "Or anybody else," he said.

There was one horrible day when a big cloud of black smoke came down on Paris and it rained black rain. That meant the invaders were here at last because the car factories outside the city were burning. Mama said it was like the end of the world with all the boots tramping everywhere, and the filthy devil's fog that was made of rubber smoke.

"The worst is that everybody's gone, run away from their own lives, nobody knows where," she said. That was frightening but she didn't mean me to hear her. She was talking to Papa in the kitchen.

Nadia and I couldn't go out to play for whole *weeks*. It was very hot and there were no lemons to make lemonade, like Mama always did in summer. All over town the shops were closed up. The Germans hung up their swastika flags everywhere you looked. They were HUGE and they made a nasty flapping sound when you had to walk under them. I said they were like pterodactyl wings but Nadia said they were like a giant's dirty washing hanging out.

"Your sister has that one right," Papa said to me.

When the Germans really got stuck in here, they put up new signposts on the main streets, all done in big black German letters. Nadia called them the witchy signposts. We had to put our clocks forward so they told the same time as Hitler's watch back in Germany. Papa set the shop wall-clock that way, but all the others he kept on French time.

Most people came back to Paris again after a while and then school started up again. They had all been somewhere in France but it didn't sound as if it had been much fun. Jean-Paul said there were planes shooting at people on the roads. He showed me how they did it.

"*Bzzzzzzzzzzzzzzzzzz* – it's like a huge mosquito, first." He buzzed around and then he banked with his arms like a plane does and made a shrieking noise in my ear. "Then the Stuka comes at you straight, like a bat out of hell. And the pilot is so close you can see his face full of hate. Then the gun goes *Da, datta, DA*. And you can see he's saying 'Ha ha, Frenchie, you're dead!'"

That wasn't fair. The people from Paris had no guns.

Jean-Paul didn't even know where he had been with his family but they lost their dog, Whistle, somewhere. That was the worst thing of all because we'd been training Whistle to walk on two legs. Now someone else has a clever dog without doing any hard work of their own.

Yes, I know. I *did* begin with the war after all. It's hard to ignore it, I suppose.

Never mind, I'll begin again tomorrow with the day my family had to move from rue de la Harpe. You can bet not everybody in the world knows about *that*. But first I have to explain about the shop and my family.

PAPA AND OUR SHOP

My father is a watchmaker and jeweller. He learned his trade in Switzerland when he was young. That's the absolute best place in the world to learn watchmaking.

Papa was born in Germany but when he was my age his family moved to Strasbourg. When he was only fourteen he took the train all the way to Geneva on his own and he became an apprentice in a famous clock-making place. They wanted him to stay because he had clever hands and could speak French and German. But Papa wanted to come back to France. And when he did, his clever hands were no use at all.

"I could make a clock for the man in the moon,"

he'd say to us. "Or a watch that would go on ticking twenty thousand leagues under the sea. But was there any work to be found in Strasbourg?"

"NO!" we had to shout back, quick as quick, because this was his joke. "So, hurry along to platform number 5, Papa. Get the fast train to Paris!"

The joke was that it was a really *good* thing there was no work for Papa because right after he got off the express train in Paris he met Mama. So it all worked out just fine. That's how our family began.

Papa made a very beautiful ring of pearls and rubies for my mother and engraved her name in fine writing along with his, on the inside. I can read it without a magnifying glass but Nadia can't.

It says: * *Anne Berlioz et Léopold Alber* * *7 January 1930.*

It's true. Mama has the same name as the famous composer Hector Berlioz. (But that is all. We are not related!) She always says that is probably why she learned to play the piano. She nearly became a famous pianist but then she got married instead.

As well as all his other jobs, Papa does some special work that he learned to do all on his own, when he was young: he makes eyes for stuffed animals and sometimes claws and beaks too, if they are missing or broken. He does this work for museums, but also for my favourite shop in Paris, Deyrolle. If you've never been there, it is like a zoo that's inside a shop. Except all the animals are stuffed.

When I was eight I was old enough to do deliveries there for Papa even though it was quite a long walk from our shop. The lady clerks and the taxidermists who stuff the animals always came over to the desk to see what I had brought. They would open the boxes in front of me and they were always delighted with Papa's work.

"Such fierce eyes!" they would say. "Perfect for our new panther." Or, "Jonas, tell us the truth. This claw is not just porcelain. Your father must have fought a grizzly bear in the park!"

That is why it was so strange later on when Signor Corrado found the pile of Deyrolle notebooks. He said they'd been left behind at the circus after a show. I don't think I had told him about the work Papa did for the shop. But when I did, all he said was, "Did I not tell you La Giaconda has great powers?"

I wonder about that.

La Giaconda is another name for the Mona Lisa, the famous painting in the Louvre. It's also another name for Signor Corrado's wife. It's her stage name. She's Italian too. But they are *not* in the war against France, like lots of Italians are.

OUR HOME

Our apartment had five full rooms on the second floor over Papa's shop on rue de la Harpe. Old Madame Perroneau lived on the first floor with her cat, Grimaldi.

My bedroom was in the front, beside Mama and Papa's, so it overlooked the street. Nadia's room was bigger than mine but all she could see was the backs of the houses behind us and all their washing, so if she was bored she'd come into mine and we would sit on the windowsill and look out.

That could be boring too, unless there was a fancy horse carriage or a brand-new American car going down the street. They did come, sometimes, because foreigners like to do that sort of thing, especially in the old narrow streets like ours. Then we'd rush down onto the street to cheer them on.

At least you can drive down rue de la Harpe, not like poor little rue du Chat-qui-Pêche, which is close by. It has nothing in it, nothing at all, and only a bicycle can ride through it. Because of its name Nadia says it should be for cats only. Especially Grimaldi, who loves fish.

Anyway, there are no foreigners now, only Germans and they don't count because they are invaders, not proper foreigners. And there are hardly any cars any more because there's very little petrol. Top brass Germans grab everything they want, so they're pretty much the only ones with big cars now. They're the ones with the medals and ribbons over their pockets who get driven everywhere.

"The ones with the golden nooses," Papa said. "The lords of misrule and destruction."

Mama said, "Shh," but Papa said nobody would know what he was talking about even if he went and shouted it outside the Hôtel Meurice, where the top brass Germans have their parties. Then she said he should think of his family if he wasn't going to think of himself. What would happen to us if he was dragged off for shouting insults at German soldiers? He didn't say anything for ages.

There *are* horses still, of course, lots of them, but they don't pull carriages any more, only delivery wagons.

MY SISTER

Nadia is only a year younger than me but I am allowed out on my own and she is not. This is not just because she is a girl and younger than me but because she is almost completely deaf, and Mama and Papa are afraid she might not hear a car coming and would get knocked down.

She used to go a special school for deaf children which is not too far from my school. She can talk pretty well and people often do not realize she is deaf, but we have to write everything down for her, or else use signs.

Mama made up a special language of signs just for Nadia when she was a baby and couldn't read. We, all of us, learned how to use it and now we can say most things we want to say to her with our hands. But she had to learn different signs when she went to school, and so did we. She can lip-read now too.

My sister can even listen to music. She would put her ear to the side of the piano when Mama played and she could tell when the music was Beethoven and when it was Chopin. Well, anybody could do that, I am sure, but Mama thinks it is very clever because Nadia's ears do not work like everybody else's.

Nadia says she likes Berlioz best but that's only because his name is the same as Mama's. I like Mozart best. Mama says when I pass my next music exams I will begin to learn either the clarinet or the flute. She'll let me choose.

But all that talk was when we had a piano, and a living room to put it in. I haven't been able to practise music for a really, *really* long time. And now, even though the Professor has his fine old piano, here I am, stuck up in the attic, like a monkey in a monkey-puzzle tree.

When I was with Signor Corrado's circus, sometimes I used to play the little organ they kept in its own little tent, but it always sounded funny. People laughed no matter what I played. They laughed most of all if I played a funeral march. Signor

Corrado said there was a clown inside the organ and he couldn't get rid of him.

I will continue my testament tomorrow because it is getting dark now. There is no special black-out bulb in this little room and the Professor told me the curtain must be pulled across all the time, even at night. I can't even have a candle in case I burn the house down.

He's just brought me up some beans and cabbage. I heard him coming so I hid the notebook. I didn't want him to see me writing anything down. He'd probably get too worried. But I wouldn't say anything bad about him, of course.

Except that the beans and cabbage were cold because this room is so far from the kitchen. Or else maybe he couldn't heat them because there was no gas. That often happens.

THE FILE WE WERE NOT ON

The Germans changed the laws of France.

Our neighbour Monsieur Zacharides said they did it just for spite because they were annoyed by the planes that came from England dropping bombs and spies. The spies had to rush off and hide their parachutes and then try to blow up the railways. But Papa said it was a much more serious plan the Germans had. He wouldn't say what, though, he just seemed to go into himself and got thin in the face. But Papa said it wasn't just spite: the Germans had a much more serious plan.

Some of the plan was just for Jews. Mama said that some people want Jews to live all together in one place. How stupid is that? But Mama said there was no need for us to worry even though we are Jewish because there was no record of us in any synagogue.

"Our identity cards say nothing about it," she said. Then she put her hand to her mouth. "You are never to repeat one word of what I just said. Do you hear me, both of you?"

Nadia and I looked at each other. Did Mama really think we talked about things like that?

But then Mama explained that after the Germans arrived we were supposed to have put our names down in some sort of file. There was a special order for all Jewish people to go along to an office and do this. But Papa didn't want to because he was born in Germany. So he thought the German army might come looking for him to join up.

When he heard we knew about the file we weren't on he roared, "Do my children think I'm going to fight against France?"

We certainly did not.

The bit about not going to the synagogue is true because neither Mama nor Papa is religious at all. My friend Jean-Paul said I was dead lucky because I didn't have to go to Mass every Sunday, or be an altar boy like him. He had to wear a kind of dress but you couldn't call it that or he got mad.

Mama said there were good bits in every religion

and it was wrong for anyone to boast that theirs was the best. Papa said she was foolish if she thought the good Catholic Führer, Herr Adolf Hitler, agreed with her on *that*. He said that being Jewish was not just about having a religion anyway, but about having a whole history.

Papa would never have said Mama was foolish before the Germans came. Nadia cried for a long time.

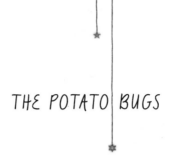

THE POTATO BUGS

At school, in the yard, we called the Germans "potato bugs" because they chewed their way through everything that was good in France and turned it all rotten.

It's a good name for them but you had to say anything like that in a low voice because walls have ears. Jean-Paul said there were German-lovers everywhere who would report you if they heard you call the soldiers "potato bug" or "Fritz".

"Then you'll be hanged from the nearest bridge and people will pelt you with rocks and dog poo," he said.

I said they wouldn't be allowed to do that to children but he got really cross with me.

"They can do what they like, pea-brain. Remember, I saw those pilots shooting people on the roads. You didn't. There were real bodies that we had to pass by. Even babies in prams. It was awful."

One of the first new laws was that there were to be two parts of France.

Potato bugs are so stupid they cannot even count on their fingers as far as Julius Caesar did. He divided France into *three* parts even though he had no trucks or tanks to get around the country in. But everyone with a brain knows that France has lots of parts!

Paris and the north are in the worst half. It has the most Germans and the most rules. People say the other part is not so bad, though Papa makes a face if anyone says "Vichy". That's the town where the French government ended up after they stopped running away from the Germans. Papa says all there is in Vichy is smelly hot baths and smelly drinking water.

"The people there must smell pretty bad too," he said.

The head of the government is old Marshal Pétain. He always wears a hat that's dripping with gold stuff. He's got more gold than any of the Germans. That's because he beat them in the really old war. But they like him anyway. Which just shows how stupid they all are.

Whenever you go to the pictures you see the Marshal. He's always up there in the newsreels, shaking hands with really clean children. They must get hot baths in Vichy because here in Paris we're filthy! We can't have baths because there's no coal to heat the water.

"Wash like Grimaldi does," Mama said. "Just watch him lick his paw and dab behind his ears."

Sometimes we use the boiled water from the vegetables. It stinks, but at least it's warm.

The only bad part about going to the pictures is that you have to watch the potato bug news-reels. The German soldiers tramp all over maps of Europe and cheer when they knock a place down. Everybody in the cinema wants to say "BOO, HISS", but you can't because then they'd turn on the lights and find out where you're sitting. Then it would be off with you to the guillotine, or some-where like that.

One time Papa looked at his watch and said it had taken nearly an hour before Robin Hood came on. To the rescue! *Tarantara!*

But we haven't been to a film for ages and ages. Jews can't go any more. That was another law they made.

WHY WE HAD TO MOVE FROM OUR HOME

Even though Paris got stuck in the worst part of France, rue de la Harpe is a good place to live. It's near the river, you can walk to the Luxembourg Gardens to play and it's got all kinds of good shops. My school is just a few streets away and Nadia's is only a bit further.

But guess what, that was *why* we had to move. The Germans don't want any Jews to have nice places to live and work in. And even though we don't go to the synagogue, they found out we were Jews anyway. We had to get new identity cards and *J* was stamped on all of them.

Mama said it was a mystery how they had found out. Papa said, "Don't be so foolish, Anne."

"I'm frightened, Léo," she said. "What you said about your cousin—"

Then she saw I was listening and she went into the kitchen. She cried and cried for ages.

The next thing was that Papa got a letter from the Germans which said our shop and quarters were to be "requisitioned". That means *stolen*. The letter said that under the new laws he was not permitted to operate his business *ever* again. It said we had to move to the fourth district and he would have to register our family there. We'd have to show our new identity papers, including proof of our *race*. The letter said Papa was lucky not to be thrown in jail, or sent away this time round, because he hadn't signed us up as Jews when the special order was made.

I know all this because Papa read the whole letter out to us. He looked like a statue when he finished. Nadia and I knew we'd better not ask any questions at *all*.

But we are French! It was hideous what they did, taking our home and our things. The potato bugs are the ones who should move. They are thieves and bullies. And invaders.

They are the enemy.

Back then, I didn't know what they meant by "this time round". Now I know.

GOODBYE TO OUR HOME

We had only one day to get ready. The most important thing was Papa's tools because he needed them in case there was any jewellery work or clock-mending where we were going. He didn't care that the new laws said he couldn't work any longer.

"They'll not take my hands away from me," he said. "Every last spanner comes along."

He put every tool in its place in the leather carry-case. His loupe eye-piece has its own velvet box and the spanners and screwdrivers fit around it like tiny knives. The loupe is my favourite of all his tools. It lets you look into a diamond and see stars.

But of course Papa couldn't take all the beautiful old clocks in the shop. He picked out all the jewels and watches that were ours and Mama wrapped them up in strips of soft chamois skin. She said we had to hide these in our clothes.

Before Papa did anything else, he wrote notes to everybody whose goods he had in the shop. He told them he was returning them now, in case they were *mislaid*. He underlined that word. I had to deliver the notes and the watches and rings to all those people who lived close by. Some of them were cross because the work wasn't finished but most were sorry to hear about our shop closing down. Later Papa went out himself on his bicycle to deliver the others. He had so many it was dark when he came home and the curfew had begun.

But there was one order from Orléans. Nobody could travel *that* far so we took it with us for safekeeping. I was glad of that because it was a microscope.

Here is a secret: a flea looks like a space monster when you put it under a microscope.

I don't know where the microscope is now but if anybody finds it in the apartment in rue des Lions it belongs to Madame Pirotte, 53 rue de la Reine Blanche, Orléans. The full address is written down under the base.

The day we moved, Papa hired a vélo taxi to bring our clothes and schoolbooks across the river. His old friend Monsieur Bambiger had buzzed around like a bumble bee and had found us an apartment.

"But it has only two rooms," Papa told us. "So you'll have to leave most of your things behind. I'm sorry. You must be brave about this, both of you."

I was allowed to bring just one storybook so I took my Alexandre Dumas omnibus which is three books in one.

Nadia took her puppet theatre. She said it folded up like a book but it was at least four times the size of my Alexandre Dumas. Papa said that was fair because Nadia is deaf and can't go out to play like me.

All the big things like cooking pots and sheets and blankets had to go inside the cabin of the vélo taxi and we were to march along behind it, with Papa wheeling his bicycle. Jews aren't supposed to have bicycles either but Papa said people could only take so much nonsense.

"Let them come and requisition the poor old bike if they want it so much," he said.

He and Mama had suitcases full of clothes and Nadia and I stuffed our school satchels with small things like pencils and needles, toothbrushes and soap. I carried the microscope in case the street cobbles shook the vélo taxi about and disturbed the lenses.

The taxi had a sign on the back which said "I'm

Yours for a Song". But that was just a joke. You have to pay the rider for all his pedalling and give him a tip if you can.

Monsieur Zacharides, who owns the Greek pastry shop two doors down on rue de la Harpe, came out to say goodbye to us. He is a big jolly man, but there he was, crying like a baby. That made it very hard for Mama, as she was trying not to cry. We all knew that leaving the piano was breaking her heart but there was nothing we could do about it so we said nothing.

Monsieur Zacharides gave Nadia a box of pastries as a treat for our first meal away from home.

He even gave the vélo man a fresh brioche. "Be careful with that luggage," he said to him. "Help my friends out when you get there. The Albers are the best neighbours in the whole world."

Madame Perroneau came down to the door and waved us off. She was crying too, into her handkerchief. That was odd because she was always the first to complain to Mama if Jean-Paul and I made too much noise outside the shop when we were racing up and down on my roller skates, or playing anything at all.

"Where's Grimaldi?" Nadia asked her.

"Oh, my pet, he's out with his lady-love from the ironmonger's shop."

Nadia nearly cried about that but she made a big effort.

"Give him my love, Madame Perroneau," she said. "Tell him to be brave always."

Other people waved at us from their shops as we passed, down as far as the dog-leg bend in the street. But Monsieur Zacharides and Madame Perroneau were the only neighbours who came out to say a proper goodbye. If there was anyone else who wanted to they were too late because we were gone.

I have written lots and lots of my Testament in just four days. There isn't much else to do here, is there?

The Professor has just left the room. He was quite nice today. He spent a lot of time up here and looked at all the books with me and asked me questions.

He didn't get near this notebook, of course. That is VERBOTEN!

"I think we'll have to draw up a proper educational plan for you, Jonas," he said. "You're a bright boy, I can see that."

I'm not sure what I think of that idea. He might get over it. Anyway he's getting more relaxed about me. And about the window.

He told me I should be able to see quite a few places if I kept well back and only peeked out by the side, right where the curtain bulges a bit.

"But don't tweak it, not even a little," he warned. "People will always spot that kind of thing out of the corner of their eye. It goes back to ancient times when we were all hunters in the forest and had to watch out for branches twitching because that could mean a tiger or a bear was lurking."

That was an interesting thing for him to say. I hadn't thought of that.

I pretended I was looking out for the first time. Rue Cuvier runs alongside the park that has the gardens *and* the zoo.

"You can't see the zoo," I told him. "Or even most of the park, but you can see people who look like they're heading for the park, or just coming out of it."

During the day children go through the park on their way to and from school. I don't know if any of them go to my school on rue Saint-Jacques. They're too far away for me to see their faces properly. They look happy enough anyway, especially when it's the right time for them to be fresh out of class. But I bet most of them don't know about the lion at the park gate.

People never look up at it. It is a complete waste

of a lion. Even if it is only a statue.

Papa first showed the lion to me when I was really small. His den is near the entrance to the park. He's up there on his own little hill and he has a great big ugly gnawed-off foot in front of him, with the toes sticking right up. Nobody knows whose foot it's supposed to be. When the war began Papa said he thought it might be Adolf Hitler's foot.

I told the Professor about that. "Papa said that would explain why the lion spat it out," I said. "Because it was so ugly. And it would explain why Hitler walked about as stiff as a poker when he came to Paris after the invasion. He was missing a foot."

Of course it was all just Papa's joke but the Prof had a really good laugh. The problem is he has this weird way of holding one hand up to his mouth as if it's a bad thing to laugh. But there's nothing wrong with his teeth. It's like he's really shy, or has forgotten how to laugh, or something.

"Did you know there's another lion up there beside yours?" he asked. "One that has only a lamb to eat, not Hitler's smelly hoof?"

But of course we did! I told him that Papa and I called it the Boring Lion.

The Prof said he was sorry he had to lock me up at the top of his house as if I was the poor old Man in the Iron Mask, but he said it was best for both of us and it wouldn't last for ever, he was sure of that.

He doesn't really lock me in. I have to say that. And he lets me go down one set of stairs to use the small toilet, though I'm not allowed to flush it. He does that afterwards with a bucket of water in case the toilet makes a noise through the walls. The Prof has his own bathroom and toilet downstairs so he says it would sound funny if he kept running upstairs to use the little one. But it's a bit awful that he has to do that.

I asked him if he'd heard any news of Mama, because he thought so well of her. This time he put both hands up to his mouth. But he wasn't laughing.

"No, Jonas," he said, "I haven't. But you know, we should never give up hope. She's in my prayers."

He said he had lit a candle in a church for all my family.

I asked him if he would play the piano and then I might be able to hear it even up here, so he said he would, tomorrow if I liked.

"But you must understand that I haven't played for a long time, Jonas." He did that throat-clearing thing again. When he hasn't got his hands up to his face he's doing that. "My wife died last Easter, you know."

How would I have known that? I didn't even know he'd had a wife.

Then he asked me what I would like to hear. I said the Brahms lullaby. "Because that would remind me of Mama. She used to sing it when she put Nadia to bed."

Nadia used to put her fingers up to Mama's mouth and throat to hear it in her own way. The words in that lullaby are the only German words I know, except for words like *heimensoldaten, kommandantur* and *verboten*. Or *jawohl!* Or *Heil Hitler!*

Jean-Paul told me that if you ever have to say that last thing, say if a German soldier puts his gun to your head or holds you out over the river and roars that he'll drop you down unless you say Heil Hitler, well, then you can say it but you must put your fingers in a *V* behind your back to take the harm away.

"*V* is for Victory," he said. "Victory for us."

The words to that lullaby sound very different from any of those words but I suppose it was written especially for babies who need soft sounds to help them go to sleep. When I go to the collège I will learn the German language anyway. Or maybe English. Papa would definitely prefer me to learn English.

Now I am a little tired of writing so I will continue the story of my family tomorrow.

Yesterday I had a fever and a bad pain in my head so I didn't write anything after all.

The Prof was out shopping or something, and I really needed a drink of water. I would have gone all the way downstairs for it, no matter what he said, but when I got out of bed and went to the door my legs were too shaky. It was like when Nadia and I had the measles last year and I couldn't walk properly. So I had to get into bed again. The Prof got an awful shock when he came up with my food.

"Look, Jonas," he whispered when he opened the door, "I've made a pancake for you. My friend who keeps a beehive nearby gave me a little honey as a treat."

Then he saw me shivering and shaking underneath the bedcover. He left the pancake on the floor and ran out and brought back a basin of cold water and a sponge. I just wanted to drink the water from the basin but he sponged me down first, like Mama did when we had measles.

Then he went downstairs and brought up a big tall cup of water and something hot in a glass that he said was a tisane. It's for fever. I drank everything and fell asleep and when I woke up it was getting dark and I was nearly better. So at least it wasn't measles again, which was good.

The pancake was cold but it was nice anyway, with the honey. The Prof looked in when I was eating it. He said he was sorry but he didn't have enough flour in the house to make another hot one. Then he said he'd leave all the doors open and play the lullaby for me downstairs. He did, and I could hear it quite well, though of course it would have been far better if we'd been in the same room. He is a really great pianist.

I think I would like him even if he didn't play well. First I thought he was too grey and quiet to like very much, but I know now he is kind. Maybe he can't help being grey and quiet. Or coughing, or moving his head that way. Maybe if he was different he wouldn't be able to play the piano like he does. But he was so good it was almost like hearing a gramophone recording, or music on the wireless. I'll ask him to play more.

THE STREET OF LIONS

Our new apartment was at 10a rue des Lions, in the fourth district. Even though Papa said it was not very far away from rue de le Harpe as the crow flies, it felt like a long walk to us because of all the stuff we had to carry. And because it was across the river. We hardly ever used to go in that direction.

Papa tried to cheer us up. He told us that long ago the old French kings used to keep their lions in a den somewhere nearby and that's how the street got its name. Nadia wanted to know if there were lions roaming around Paris back then, like cats, but Mama said the place was probably just a kind of zoo the kings had. I would say the kings used to run proper gladiator games with the traitors and spies they had back then. They would have learned how to do that from the ancient Romans. But I wonder where they got the lions.

Anyway, the bad thing was the street looked very dull and quiet, not interesting like its name. Nor like rue de la Harpe either. There was no shop at No. 10a, just a boarded-up front window where there had been a shop years ago. Papa had to knock because we didn't have a key. After a long time a very old woman opened the door and Papa explained that we were going to live on the top floor and that his friend had made all the arrangements with her husband. She was very deaf so he had to shout but it was only at about the third time shouting that she heard him at all. People in the next houses were opening their windows to see what the noise was all about.

"Léo, we'll need a front door key at once because that poor woman is failing," Mama whispered, even though the woman was deaf. "Get one quickly."

The three of us went upstairs while Papa waited and tried to get a key from the old woman.

We knew there would be only two rooms but we hadn't expected them to be so small. They were both at the back, like Nadia's room at rue de la Harpe, but hers was bigger than either of these. The windows were dirty but Mama said the floors had good wood in them. "And there's nothing so bad that some elbow grease won't shift it."

There were two beds in one room but she said that she and Papa would need one of them. She said they'd keep it in the other room for daytime use, as if it was a sofa, because that room would have to be their bedroom and our living room and kitchen all in one.

"You two will have to share this room and take turns with the bed. One week one of you will have the bed and the other one can sleep on cushions on the floor. It'll be fine. It'll be like camping."

How would Mama know *that*? We'd never gone camping in our whole lives.

Papa had the key by then so we all got to work cleaning the place up and he went off looking for water.

It was on the next floor down but there was only a trickle in the tap. Papa told us when he came back with half a bucket of water. "The toilet has to do five families," he said. "I think mostly we'll be using this very bucket, or something like it."

Mama looked like a statue when he said that but we knew she was upset. So were we. It was not very nice to hear something like that.

We worked really hard to clean the floors and the windows but most of the dirt on the windows was outside. "Pure grime," Mama said. Nadia said it might be lion spit from years ago but I told her that was just silly.

"Lions can climb," she said. "Silly *you* not to know that."

I would have quite liked to have stood on the windowsill and scrubbed the glass from outside but Mama wouldn't let me. I reckoned because we were so high up I would be able to see the river bending around like it does in the maps in geography class. I even thought I might be able to see rue de la Harpe too, and be able to keep an eye on our place, even though it was on the other side of the river.

But we never saw our home again after that. Even I didn't, not even when I was out and about. That's because the fairground is on the same side of the river as rue des Lions but away to the east, at Nation. And Papa made me promise I wouldn't cross the river again.

If the Prof is going to be kind like he was yesterday I might ask him if he wouldn't mind taking a walk in the direction of rue de la Harpe to see if our shop looks all right. It's not too far away from this house so he wouldn't get too tired.

MORE GERMAN RULES: PARKS VERBOTEN!

I will make up for the day I didn't write by explaining about some of the new German laws. Most of them seemed to be about things Jews couldn't do.

When we were settled into the apartment in rue des Lions, Papa told us that the reason we were forced to move from our home was because of pure spite on somebody's part.

"As your mother knows by now, spite is a bottomless well," he said. "Then there's all that German paperwork that catches people out. Between them that's what's put the Alber family in the soup this time."

I'm not sure what he meant. I think somebody reported we were Jews who hadn't put their names on that stupid file. But why would they go and say that to the Germans? If you're French you shouldn't say anything to them.

One of the really worst laws they passed said that Jews couldn't go to parks or use public telephones. Also, if you had to shop you could only do it between three and four o'clock. But most shops are closed then! And what would Papa have done if he was still in his own shop? Would he have to do all his work between those times and then go and drink tea for the rest of the time? We thought it was a very, *very* stupid law.

"If we try to go into a park how will the Germans know we are Jews, anyway?" Nadia asked Papa.

It sounded like a baby question but actually it was clever. Except that the mean old potato bugs thought of it in the end. Though it took them a long time. They didn't figure it out until just a few months ago.

PAPA, MAMA, NADIA AND ME: THE SCIENTIFIC FACTS

Papa is a man of average size but Mama is very, *very* small, just about 150 centimetres tall. Papa calls her a pocket treasure. Even when she wears her funny high heels made of cork she only comes up to his clavicle.

"Look, your mother *still* only comes up to my clavicle! We'll have to send her back along with the geraniums that didn't grow last year either!"

That's what he said on her last birthday. Mama thumped him but it was just pretend.

"Clavicle" sounds like a musical instrument but it's a bone. The collarbone. Papa always uses the proper words for things. I like that.

Anyway, Nadia is small just like Mama, but it

doesn't really matter that much for a girl.

The unfortunate truth is that I am small too. For my age, at least. Here is a confession: I won't be ten until October but I wrote down "ten" in my will anyway because it looks better to have an age in double figures.

I still wear short pants all the time even though Jean-Paul was already into his longs last year. That's what you have to wear in the collège but Mama says there was no chance of me having anything new to wear for a long time, short or long.

She says not to worry, that I'll soon grow tall enough, like Papa, but it's hard to grow now because the food is so terrible. You need meat and butter and eggs to get taller but we only have turnips and cabbage soup and nasty black bread. We don't even get the yucky vitamin pills any more because they're given out in school.

And guess what, Nadia and I have had no schools to go to since we moved. Papa was considering whether to enrol us in the nearby school, on rue Vieille du Temple, but he said he'd really prefer to keep us away from roll-books and all official things like that.

"I want to keep them away from the spotlight," he said to Mama one night in the other room. I could hear him even though his voice was low. "Out of harm's way, as much as we can manage it. I don't like it one bit that they've corralled so many families all around here. They want to know where we are, all the time. They've counted us, how many times now? And why is that?"

He told us he was quite sure that between them he and Mama could teach us very well on their own. I bet Jean-Paul would think we were lucky not to have to go to school but I wasn't so sure it was a good idea. There are lots of things about school you miss when you can't go any more. Your friends, mostly. Football. Swapping things.

Anyway, because we're not so tall, Nadia and I, Mama was trying to keep our J1 food coupons going as long as she could. You get allowed more food if you are a J1 child than nearly anybody else does, except, of course, the fat potato bugs. They get all the meat they want, *plus* cream and butter. Babies get quite a bit too, even though they're French.

Mama said that lots of the shopkeepers don't look properly at a child's papers to see the real age before they stamp them, but this only happens if the children come along with the mother and look the right age. She did her best but in the end she had to make me a J2. J1s are only for children up to six years of age. I hated being a pretend J1 until I was nearly eight. Anyway, it didn't matter by then because Jews weren't allowed to queue for food any more.

But last June, when the new law about the yellow stars came in, then, even though I was officially a J2, Mama thought she would try to keep both of us under the age for wearing *them* too.

HOW THE GERMANS GOT TO KNOW WHO IS JEWISH — AND HOW WE LEARNED TO FOOL THEM

Ever since this summer began, every person who is Jewish has had to wear a yellow Star of David sewn onto their coats all the time. That's the law. *But not if you are under six.*

Nadia definitely looks like she could be that young. But there is no way I do. It is an insult even to think it. I am a full J2.

I had a really bad argument with Mama about it. She was sitting in our living room, sewing the stars onto her and Papa's clothes. They are huge things, about the size of Papa's fist, and "JEW" is printed across the middle in black German letters like those on the signposts. You have to use up your own clothing coupons to buy them, which is the meanest thing of all.

The law says that Jews have to have the yellow stars on all their jackets and coats, both the winter ones and the summer ones, so that French people and Germans can see they are Jews, all the year round. But we are *French!* How stupid can they be?

I bet I know what Jean-Paul would say about that. He'd say the Germans should wear hairy potato bugs on their coats, with vampire teeth sticking out. He used to draw them like that on his copybooks. But we can see who's German anyway, because they wear uniforms, even the women, so there's no point.

Anyway, Mama said she and Papa would wear the stars since they had no choice because of where we were living now, where nearly everyone wore a star, but Nadia and I should not.

"I'll be struck down before I'll sew those filthy things on your innocent little garments," she said. She looked furious, but because she had a star in one hand and a needle and thread sticking out of her mouth, she sounded a little bit funny.

"Jonas, don't you see it's a way of fighting them back if you don't wear one? I *know* you could get away with it. You're small enough."

She said the Germans' law wouldn't work the way they wanted if I did that. And then, just like

Papa wanted, we'd be well away from the spotlight.

"It'll be a secret weapon. A disguise that isn't a disguise," she said. "You'll be like a spy."

I reminded her that everybody in our building in rue des Lions was Jewish and the Germans knew we were too because they'd made us come here and had stamped our papers with the *J*.

"And if we go out walking with you and Papa and you're wearing the stars people will know we're Jews too because we're your children."

That was so obvious. Why was she being so silly?

"So we *still* won't be able to go into the parks unless you stay outside and peek through the railings at us as if we're animals in the zoo. Anyway, somebody would see you watching us and so they'd know right well we're Jews too."

But Mama said I was far too logical, just like Papa, and it drove her crazy.

"You should do this one thing for me. And you can't make me sew anything onto your clothes, Jonas. I'll just drop my needle and thread on the floor right now and there they'll stay till the war's over. So there!"

She did just that too. She threw down the needle and thread.

I asked her did she think her son was some sort

of dwarf, and she began to cry. It was just as well Papa was out because he would have been furious with me for getting Mama into a state.

In the end we fixed on a bargain. She sewed a star on my winter coat, which is far too small for me now anyway. Dwarf or not, I don't think I'll be wearing it when it gets cold again. Anyway, I don't have it here. But she didn't sew stars onto my other clothes. And Nadia didn't mind at all that she had no star.

I was glad she didn't have one when I saw poor little Giselle Bauer from the apartment on the ground floor wearing a star on her silly-frilly white dress. It looked horrible, as if someone had come right up and stood in front of her and thrown a dirty rotten goose egg straight at her heart.

2 SEPTEMBER 1942

HERE IS AN ANNOUNCEMENT

We've been at war for nearly three years. The Prof told me that last night when he brought up my food, but I knew it anyway. Nobody in France is ever, *ever* going to forget the date of 3 September 1939, not even babies. We declared war on Germany that day. It's like 14 July only it's the dead opposite. It's a black day, not a blue-white-red one. No fireworks. Just nasty blue light bulbs and a curfew instead. And mountains of turnips.

And boys shut up at the top of strange houses. Maybe there are other boys living all over Paris in little rooms like this one. Who knows?

It's now much more than six weeks since I last saw Mama, Papa and Nadia. The date was 15 July.

They were all taken away somewhere on 16 July. Somewhere in France.

In all that time nobody has ever been able to tell me any more than that. But then the only people I've talked to since then are the Corrados, the other people at the fair and the Prof. And sometimes I think he knows more than he's letting on.

I wonder if he has a proper wireless set. That's how you get to know things.

One thing we really missed when we moved to rue des Lions was our wireless set. Because guess who isn't allowed to have a wireless:

No. 1 – Germans

No. 2 – Marshal Pétain

No. 3 – Jews

Not so hard, huh?

Anyway, Papa left our wireless set with Monsieur Zacharides. It was a really good one too. It got all the stations you ever wanted.

Here is an announcement: everybody in France is supposed to have their wireless tuned to TSF or Radio Paris so they can hear all the stupid potato bug news and their stupid potato bug music. But nobody does *that*.

When it gets dark and you have to pull your curtains for the blackout everyone turns their wireless on. You watch the screen light warm up until you can read the names of all the cities in Europe. And even Istanbul, which is in Asia. Then when the wireless set is good and hot and working properly everyone turns the sound down really low and twists the dial all the way round to London. London sends out the proper French news. The French people living there tell the truth. They know about all the battles the Germans are losing and getting killed in, stuff we never hear about. Ha ha – now we do.

When the news is over they send out all the spy messages. They're the best. Stuff like "The cocoa is getting cold". Or "Madeleine has no cigarettes to-night". Or "The wolf has bitten the lamb in three places".

But every word means something special to someone, somewhere. It's a code that tells that person what they should go and do next. Maybe blow up another train or put sugar in German petrol tanks so they can't move their trucks.

One day Nadia made up a play that was full of spy messages, after I explained to her what they were. She had her king and queen and the princesses and the fairies and even old Puss in Boots running about the stage, shouting out stuff about the lambs drinking the cocoa, and giants sharpening their razors on Madeleine's hatpin.

It was crazy but it was funny too. Mama said

she had a great imagination. Jean-Paul heard her at it one day but he just thought she was mad. He was silly sometimes.

There are lots of French people in England, Papa says. They escaped, but one day they're going to come back here with an army, and American soldiers and English soldiers will come too. The Germans had better look out then because all those soldiers will be really angry about all the bad things that have happened here since the war began. And they'll have bombs and tanks and stuff because the radio people in London will make sure they get everything they need. Colonel de Gaulle is the boss over there, Papa says.

Sometimes I think maybe Mama and Papa and Nadia escaped after all. Nadia has her great imagination. She'd be able to make up a story that would fool any stupid German. They could have gone south, over the No-No line, to the other part of France, where there are hardly any Germans bossing people around.

But I know they wouldn't have tried to escape unless I was with them, so I suppose they just didn't, and that's that.

GATHERING WINTER FUEL

My teacher, Monsieur Lemoine, would be cross with me. I've just read back the last few pages and I can see I am not composing this story the way he likes, with a Beginning, a Middle and an End.

I really *do* think it's good advice but:

No. 1 – It's not always easy to see where things should go in a story when you're getting it all down.

No. 2 – Sometimes you remember a thing suddenly, and it's best to put it in right away or you might forget it. And it's something you would really miss.

I don't want to forget anything. But sometimes I get confused about which thing happened before which other thing. Like the different laws for Jews, because there are so many of them, and even though they are all awful they got worse.

But I know for sure we were in rue des Lions for the whole of last winter. I remember that because we all spent days in bed trying to keep warm and not grow an appetite.

"When they're not starving us they're trying to freeze us to death," Mama said. "But we'll show them."

We weren't growing but we weren't exactly starving. We were hungry. But you can get very tired of turnips and watery beetroot soup.

Only Papa went out. Every morning, after one cup of the stinky coffee made of roots that hasn't even *one* coffee bean in it, he went out to the parks, looking for logs or twigs for our fire.

"It's bloody hard work to find anything bigger than a match," he said. Mama made a face because of his bad language but he didn't care. "Everyone in Paris is up at the crack of dawn with a fine-tooth comb, crawling under the trees."

So, after a while Papa took to going quite a long way on his bicycle, past the city ring road, which is pretty far. Then he would walk along the railway lines. This was *so* much against the law. Twice over.

No. 1 – Jews were not allowed to go more than five miles from their home.

No. 2 – *Nobody* was supposed to go near the train tracks anyway. VERBOTEN.

But what else could Papa do? There was much more wood and brambles and stuff to be had along the railway.

"Nothing is impossible for a willing heart," Mama said, every time he went out. She always used to say that to encourage us, even before the war. But there were deep lines all around her mouth until Papa got home again. Nadia tried to smooth them out with her fingers but it didn't work.

The best thing about Papa going along the tracks was that sometimes he found little rough pieces of coal that had fallen from the train tenders.

He used to bring a sack and scissors, and heavy gloves for the brambles. One day when the snow had gone I went with him.

THE DAY PAPA AND I
WENT OUT TOGETHER

Papa said he would bring me out with him because: No. 1 – I was getting too pasty being inside and No. 2 – I was giving Mama too much cheek.

"I don't mind that, Léo," she said. "For heaven's sake, leave the boy here where he's safe."

"He has to learn," said Papa. "He has to know what to do, just in case."

He didn't say what just in case meant. But we all knew it would be something bad. Lots of French men were sent off to work in Germany because the German men were away fighting. If that happened to Papa…

When we got up on the bike he folded his sack to make a kind of cushion on the crossbar. But

I could still feel the cold on my bottom. My legs were frozen, even though Mama had done her best and knitted long socks for me and Nadia with wool from an old cardigan.

Long ago Papa would put me on the crossbar and Nadia on the carrier, and we would whizz along the best boulevards until we spotted an ice cream van and then we'd stop. Chocolate for me, vanilla for Papa and Nadia.

But when we left rue des Lions that day there was no whizzing, and you can bet there was no ice cream either. I could hear Papa puffing really hard, even though there was no Nadia. We had to stop a few times and wait until he got his breath back. He said he was out of practice having a passenger on board. He said I must have put on weight.

"But only in your liver or some other hidden part of you because the rest of you is still as skinny as one of my old Auntie Gertrud's chickens."

"If only you'd had some real coffee, you'd be like a racer, Papa," I said.

He made a face. "So, let's go and see if there's any wood left in the forest," he said. That was meant to be a joke so I laughed. We got back on the bike.

Papa's plan that day was to head for the park at Vincennes, not to follow the train tracks. I was disappointed. I thought if we went along the tracks we just might get lucky and see a train being blown to bits by the train saboteurs. I didn't say that, though.

However, it was just as well we went the way we did. That's for sure.

We got to the big round space at Place de la Nation and Papa swung himself off the bike. There was more noise than I could believe. I don't know where those people had got their petrol from, but there was a lot of traffic. It was mostly German army trucks, stuffed with potato bugs and their guns, but there were quite a few cars too. Some of them had funny gas tanks on the roof. There were motorbikes too, smelly and smoky. And lots of vélo taxis.

One poor Citroën with a funny petrol tank, like a bottle stuck to the radiator, suddenly drifted to the side and halted, right in front of us. Papa stopped me staring at the people inside by pulling me away from the kerb.

"Mind yourself, son!" he said, really loud. He was holding me so tight it hurt. Then, when we were well away from the car, he spoke with his teeth closed together. "Didn't I warn you not to draw any attention to us?"

I said I was sorry. But the car stopping wasn't my fault.

We crossed all the avenues. It took us ages to get to the big wide one called Cours de Vincennes. It has two statues standing on great tall columns on either side of the road. They look like Romans but Papa says they're French kings. Anyway, when you see them you know you have arrived at the fairground, the Foire du Trône.

And there was *still* a fair there, just where I remembered, from the time before the Germans. We used to come every summer.

Maybe there weren't as many stands or carousels as there used to be but there was a string of bunting between the trees, and some coloured flags flying. There were vans parked in a line, stretching down the avenue. But since nobody in a fair gets up early in the morning all the van doors were closed.

Except one.

HOW I MET SIGNOR CORRADO
AND LA GIACONDA

Papa was just about to lift me back onto the crossbar when I left him standing there. I just had to.

"I'll only be a minute!" I shouted back at him. "Just wait!" I didn't stop to hear if he said anything. I had to see IT close up before it broke up.

IT = THEM.

Outside the big yellow van whose door was open there were two people on a bright green deckchair, as if it was summer. The two of them were on the same chair. One was sitting the ordinary way people sit. He was a man dressed in a Pierrot costume with a big red bow at the neck and he was smoking a cigarette. The other person was standing upside down on his head.

Actually, I don't know whether you can say "standing" if the person is upside down. Maybe there's another word.

The upside down one was a woman and she was wearing a long black striped costume with legs, a bit like an old-fashioned bathing suit. She had lots of black curly hair but it was spread out on top of his, like a wig. Like him, she was smoking, only not a cigarette – a big fat cigar.

They both looked really comfortable.

I could hear Papa calling me back but now that I'd got up close I wasn't going to go away without a proper look. Besides, it would do his wheezing good if he took a rest.

"Hello, boy," said the woman. She could see me coming even though we were upside down to each other. "Are you useful?"

"Yes," I said. What else could I say?

"Then please go inside the caravan and fetch me my mirror," she said. "You'll find it on the table in the kitchen."

I did what she asked. The van had a set of little wooden steps with flowers painted on them. It was quite roomy inside, and whoever lived in it had made different rooms by hanging curtains from one side to the other. They were printed with stars.

I knew the room I'd walked into was the kitchen

because there was a small fat stove with a frying pan on it, and a small dresser with cups and plates, all in bright colours. There was a round table opposite the door with a beautiful silver hand mirror on it.

I brought it out to the woman. She took it and held it by the handle with the right side up. Of course, for her that would have been the wrong side. The man said nothing, just puffed on his cigarette, but he had a nice smiling kind of face. He was very dark-skinned.

I looked around for Papa but he was just standing by the footpath, holding his bike.

"I was right, Luigi," the woman said, after a minute or two. "I *do* look like our very own Mona Lisa when I am upside down. It's the way my mouth goes. I can't think why you haven't noticed before now."

Then she suddenly did a flip. Or maybe there's another word for what she did, some word that only circus people know. I've never asked. Anyway, she managed to knock herself off the man's head. She ended up standing on her feet beside me, with the cigar still burning away, like the ones cowboys in the pictures have.

She held out her left hand to me and I took it. I could see that she was not as young as she had looked when she was upside down. She was probably around Mama's age. But who could imagine Mama upside down on top of Papa's head, smoking a cigar?

"You have the honour of meeting La Giaconda, boy," she said. "Mona Lisa, if you prefer. Yesterday I was plain Lucia, but now the whole of Paris lies at my feet."

"Never plain," said the man. "That, never."

"I'm Jonas," I said to the woman, because she was still holding my hand. "I'm pleased to meet you."

Out by the roadside Papa gave a roar so I knew I had to go.

"Your father?" asked the man. I nodded. "Well, Jonas," he said. "Since you were here to witness the magical transformation of my wife into La Giaconda, a real live Italian work of art, why don't you and your father come and see our show tomorrow afternoon? You would be most welcome."

He spoke French, but not like anybody I knew. His voice seemed to have the sun in it, just like his face did, and his teeth, which were really white. He spoke every word slowly and smoothly, as if he was spinning sugar on a stick.

I don't know why I said what I said next.

Mama had warned us never to say anything about ourselves.

"But we're Jewish," I said. "I don't think we can come."

Then I remembered my manners. "But thank you very much."

The man sat up straight, as if the deckchair had suddenly grown a long stiff back. He took the cigarette from his mouth, stubbed it out and put it in his pocket. Then he stood up.

"In that case, Jonas," he said, "I promise that you will have the best ringside seats."

He made a little face.

"Well, that is, you would have them, if we *had* a ring," he said. "But you will have the best of what the Corrado Circus has to offer. And if you have any brothers or sisters or cousins or any companions in crime like yourself, bring them too. Your party will be our most honoured guests."

FEASTS

Today is the war's third birthday. The Prof made scrambled eggs for us. He said they weren't hen eggs *exactly* but they had just the same kind of protein inside them that would make me grow. When I asked if they were magpie eggs he just laughed.

"I've a source not so far away that sometimes comes up trumps," he said. "It's like having shares in a shipping line. Of course, I refer to the days when shares used to come up trumps."

I didn't know about that, but for someone who is so shy he seems to know quite a few people who give him things. Maybe they were once his pupils, like Mama was.

Anyway, the eggs were delicious even though

there was too much pepper in them. I didn't even mind that the bread wasn't toasted, because the eggs took the staleness out of it. But I don't know why he wouldn't say what kind of eggs he'd used. Were they dinosaur eggs? The museum is just across the park. But I didn't say that in case it sounded like the eggs were bad.

He brought everything up to my attic room – the pot with the eggs, the bread, the plates – and he ate here with me, both of us sitting on the floor with our backs to the bed. That's the first time he's done that. Really, I'd much prefer to go downstairs and eat with him in his kitchen but maybe this was a start.

"It makes a change to eat with somebody else," I said. "I like it better."

He coughed for a bit about that. Then he told me that he and his wife have a son called Robert, but he lives in the United States of America. They were going to go there to be with him, just before the Germans came, but then Madame Prof got ill and so they couldn't go. Then she died. He said Robert plays the violin in an orchestra in New York, so that means he must be an adult, not a child. The Prof is definitely too old to be a child's father.

I feel bad sometimes that I'm getting better food here than I did in rue des Lions. Mama did her best but there was very little she could find for us. And because Papa couldn't work, at first there was only the little bit of money he had left from the shop.

It was Nadia who saw Papa going to where he'd hidden the stuff we'd brought with us, the watches and jewels wrapped up in the chamois skins. He'd made a safe place for them under the floorboards. Nadia saw him take two watches out and put them in his pocket. She can be really quiet when she wants and people sometimes forget she is there.

Papa must have, that day at least. He wrote a note for Mama and left it by the sink. Then he went out.

When he came back he had some fish, red mullet I think it was, and some bread that was *nearly* white. Well, at least it wasn't black with spots in it, like the usual bread. He had some big green apples too, eggs, a bag of flour and a tiny tub of butter.

"Well, you know I can't make an apple tart," Mama said. "We've no oven, only that useless fireplace. So don't you people get your hopes up too high."

But she was smiling. She made pancakes with apple sauce instead. You see? She always does her best.

You'd have thought Papa would be really happy that he was able to bring back some really nice food that day, just like in the old times. But no, his face was like thunder. I heard him mutter something to Mama about enjoying the food because there wouldn't be much more like it.

"I got a miserable price from someone I trusted," he said. "They have us over a barrel."

I guessed the food had been very dear, wherever he'd bought it. You could see it was black market stuff, the kind that comes up from the country, or from somewhere that isn't ordinary. Black market stuff is always dear because you can't use your food coupons.

But when we were in our room that night Nadia told me about Papa taking the watches out of the hiding place. She said he must have sold them. Of course she hadn't heard what he'd said at dinner, so I didn't tell her. She was still so happy about the pancakes.

She said there must be at least ten more watches left in the safe place. "Because I carried six and so did you. I don't know how many rings there are. Enough for years, I bet."

The next chance I got I lifted the floorboard and counted them. There were twenty-two rings left.

LESSONS

Nadia was a year older than Giselle Bauer but she used to play with her anyway, even though Giselle didn't really understand about Nadia being deaf. She kept yammering away, like a stupid little budgie in a cage, just baby stuff and doll stories. It drove Mama mad to listen to her, never mind me.

It was a funny thing but right where we lived on rue des Lions all the other children were girls – or boys who were very young, just babies, really. I had nobody to play with. Mama began to say things about me going to school after all because I needed the company, but Papa was dead set against it. He had a notion something would happen to me there and he wouldn't be able to stop it.

He began to teach me some mathematics, and even a bit of chemistry, which only happens when you go to the collège. Except we didn't have any materials, just flour and salt, cooking things like that.

"What about our gold and silver?" I asked. "They're elements. Couldn't we do something with them?"

Papa had shown me their names on the periodic table of the elements. Gold is *Au*; silver is *Ag*. I thought it was a smart idea but he just got cross.

"Don't be silly, Jonas," he said. "Just learn the names. It's a start."

He wasn't a bad teacher but he wasn't as good at explaining things as Mama was. She told great stories. I suppose it's easier to tell stories when the lessons are about history and books. Mama was very good at giving descriptions of people from history, like Vercingétorix and Roland, who were great French fighters. And she was really sorry for poor Napoléon, cruelly locked up on his island in the middle of the ocean.

"Maybe he had a cat for a friend," Nadia said. "Or hens."

Mama also told us proper stories that she remembered. Some were written by Charles Dickens, who was English, and some came from the *Arabian Nights*. She read out bits from the book she'd brought with her from rue de la Harpe, *Les Misérables*, and made me and Nadia copy them out, to practise our handwriting and spelling. But there was no paper so we had to use the back pages in our school books. My eraser was just about rubbed out with all the work it had to do.

I think what upset Mama most was that I had no music. So she made me sing scales and taught me all the songs she knew.

"Remember, your voice is an instrument too." she said. "So learn to use it."

I don't have a great voice, though. Not like Jean-Paul. Everyone thought he sounded like an angel. He even looked like one because his hair was fair and curly. Monsieur Lemoine used to say that Jean-Paul's angel voice was proof that God has a sense of humour.

I really missed Jean-Paul. I even missed Vincent Bel, who used to follow the two of us around like a puppy. If there'd been another boy living on the rue des Lions we could have had some fun together, even if there was nothing to swap any more, no comics, no sweets.

But there's always a silver lining. My Granny Berlioz used to say that before she died. I suppose her silver lining was that she escaped the war and the bad stuff by dying first.

6 SEPTEMBER 1942

It's been nearly eight weeks now and there's still no word from my family. I know Mama and Papa would send a letter or a card to *somebody* if they could let me know where they are.

I don't know if the people at the fairground can get letters like normal people do. If I were a postman I bet it would be a lot more fun to deliver a letter to a circus van than to a boring lot of letterboxes. And circus dogs don't bite. They just snore.

I'm thinking about asking the Prof to go to Signor Corrado to ask if there's been a letter for me. But you couldn't really imagine him ever going near a fairground. And he's already done me one favour.

He went to see the shop in rue de la Harpe. He said it was open.

"It's actually still a jewellery business," he said. "Though, more accurately, a pawnbroker's shop. It's called 'The Viscount' now, I'm afraid."

Stupid name!

"Are the grandfather clocks and the carriage clocks still in the window?" I asked.

He looked a bit confused and then he coughed. "I didn't see any clocks, Jonas. Just some small items."

"Never mind," I said. "They were probably moved to the storeroom."

I didn't want him to feel bad, but I was pretty sure the Germans had looted them, just like Papa said they would if he wasn't there to protect them.

I can't sleep very well. It's not just because of the planes going over at night. It's not even the stuffy air in this room. And it's not because of the German patrols tramping past either, though there are definitely more of them on this street than you'd ever have around rue des Lions.

I just have a bad feeling in my stomach. It gets worse at night when I can't see anything from the window. It's getting dark earlier now and I'm fed up with the dark.

I really hate this room now. Yesterday the Prof

gave me a brush and a dustpan to use and clean sheets to put on the bed. He said he had a whole linen cupboard full of clean sheets and we might as well use them up.

"Don't you think it would be a good idea to do a clean up, Jonas? You do your room and I'll do mine and we'll feel better afterwards."

But there was no dirt, not that I could see. Well, there was one spider's web in the corner beside my bed but I left it alone. Why would I knock a spider's house down? She probably thinks this room is a great place to live, and the war is great because there are no more vacuum cleaners going around trying to suck her up.

Here's what I would say to Lady Spider if I could speak Spider: "This is definitely *not* a great place, because there's nobody here but *me*."

The Prof has been out of the house quite a lot for the past few days. He has to judge piano exams. The people at the Conservatoire asked him to come back and do that, even though he's retired. He put a suit on so it must be important.

"It'll be a little extra money for us," he said. "I'll look out for something tasty to bring home if they pay me on the spot."

Imagine, every month he has food coupons to spare! That's one thing we never had, that's for sure. Maybe he hasn't told them his wife is dead and so he can get hers too.

It's funny the way you know a house is empty. When there is someone in the house, even if the other person is sleeping and everything is quiet, you know they're there and it feels all right even if it's boring. But when there's no sound at all except from outside, especially when it gets dark and all you can hear is army boots going *tramp, tramp, tramp, tramp, tramp,* well, then it's completely different.

"GONE, GONE, GONE, GONE, GONE."

That's what the boots are saying.

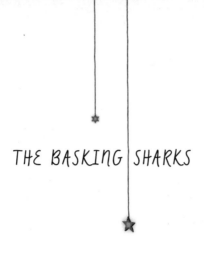

THE BASKING SHARKS

If Nadia was here I would tell her about the basking sharks. She'd love them. We could put on a play with basking sharks and pretend her theatre had got flooded because it had a river underneath it, like the deep black river that flows under the Paris Opéra House. Mama told us about that. It's even got fish in it.

Today I read about the basking sharks in the Professor's encyclopedia. That was before I got fed up with reading. Or before it got dark anyway.

Basking sharks are the biggest sharks in the world but they don't eat people at all. They're more like big vacuum cleaners. They just drift around the Atlantic Ocean and suck up every scrap of food they can see. Only they don't even have to look for the food, they just open their mouths and everything floats into it. It goes straight down into their liver which is the size of a football field, or something nearly that big.

Maybe it was a basking shark that swallowed the Jonas in the Bible. Not a whale, like it says. Old Jonas probably didn't know the difference anyway. Mama says they called me after him, No. 1 – because he was a great survivor, but really No. 2 – because they liked the name. So do I. It's not a boring name like Henri or Georges.

It was the sharks' enormous mouths I loved best. The encyclopedia had a good picture. They gape open and look like métro tunnels. They don't have teeth, like other sharks. If you could fit a basking shark into the Deyrolle shop and hang it from the ceiling it would be the best thing they ever had. And Papa could do a really good job making big round eyes for it.

Only it's just too bad for the basking sharks that everybody wants their oil. The fishermen in Ireland go out on the ocean in tiny boats that look like baskets. They harpoon the sharks and drag them over to the nearest beach and then cut out their livers. Then the livers are sent off somewhere and squeezed like oranges to get the oil out. Cities used to use that oil for street lights in the last century. Now there are no proper street lights. I suppose the basking sharks can be happy about that, even if nobody else is.

I'll ask the Prof if he knows about them when he comes home. I'll sit on the top step outside the toilet so he'll see me when he comes upstairs to go to bed.

THIS IS THE LAST CHAPTER
OF THE FIRST BOOK

There are just a couple of pages left in this notebook so I'll fill them up and then I'll begin a new one. And this time I will definitely keep to Monsieur Lemoine's rules of writing: BEGINNING, MIDDLE, END. I'm not sure about today's date but I know it's the tenth week anyway because I've made nine notches on the leg of the bed. I was pretty good at keeping the score until last week, when I couldn't stop thinking about bad things.

On the really awful night, the Prof came home and found me on the stairs. He had to pick me up and bring me to bed, but I wouldn't let him go. I couldn't. I kept my arms clasped around his neck as if he was Papa. But the Prof is so old I could hear his heart going *boom-boom*. He had to lie down with me until I went to sleep.

The next day he told me we couldn't go on like this for ever.

"I can't forget the way I found you, Jonas, curled up and whimpering like a puppy. You could have fallen down the stairs and broken your neck."

I think he's making a plan but he hasn't told me anything. I suppose that's in case it doesn't happen. And I don't know if I want anything else anyway. It might be worse.

The Prof doesn't have a wireless but he does have a wind-up gramophone. So, it wouldn't matter if there was no electricity, you could still use it. I saw it in his bedroom, on the next floor down. It was on top of one of the bedside cabinets.

It's *really* old-fashioned. It has a big horn, like an elephant's ear or something. It looks exactly like the one in the dog record label. Everyone knows that label. The dog in the picture got an awful shock one day long ago when he heard his master's voice coming out of the machine. He cocked his ear to listen, and that made him famous.

The Prof doesn't really seem to bother much about music any more unless I ask him to play. I don't know why that is. If I could play as well as he does I would get up on the stage and play and make people happy.

I must remember to ask the Prof what the date is because I don't like not knowing it. After all, guess who's going to be ten on 15 October 1942?

NOTEBOOK

2

6 MARCH: DOUBLE DATE!

The day I met the Corrados, Papa didn't say much when I got back to where he was standing with his bike, looking cross. Not even when I told him that we'd just been given a personal invitation to the circus. Papa just said we'd better push on with the job we had or there'd be an iceberg in the grate instead of a fire.

We didn't find too many good sticks that day. I climbed up pretty high in some of the trees at Vincennes, and broke off branches and twigs for Papa to pick up. But every bit of wood near the bottom of the trees was already gone. Cleared out. You'd think a brontosaurus had just gone by that morning, munching his way through it all.

I saw some magpie nests up higher, which would have been really great to burn. It wouldn't have been mean because there wouldn't be any eggs in them yet and the magpies could sleep on top of buildings instead. But when Papa saw me looking at them he shouted at me to come down.

When we arrived back home and I told Mama about the circus she got really excited.

"Aren't you my great fellow, Jonas!" she said to me. "I always love a circus. That is so exciting!"

But Papa said she shouldn't get wound up about a bit of tinsel tat.

"Anyway, we're forbidden to go to a film or a play," he said. "Do you think a circus is any different?"

"But they *said* they wanted us, Papa," I said. "The man said he would give us the best seats."

If we didn't go – well, I didn't know what I'd do.

Mama just made a face right back at him. "So what if you and I have to stand by the side of the road?" she said. "At least let the children have a treat. We're all sick and tired of living here like mice in a wall."

Nadia was so thrilled she said nothing at all. That's what she's like. She goes into herself like Papa, but only about good things. He does it about bad things. Mama and I are a bit like each other.

When we get excited we talk all the time and we never think something just isn't going to turn out well in the end.

The really good thing was that the day we were invited was Nadia's birthday. That was 6 March. She was eight years of age on the Sunday we went to the circus. And if we hadn't gone, the truth is there wasn't really going to be anything very much for her, except for what Mama had made for her during the week. Which was a new actor for her theatre.

She made his body out of some nice smooth cardboard she found on a window ledge on the landing and she made his costume out of an old tie of Papa's that she couldn't get the stains out of. She drew a face on him and stuck a little clipping of her own hair to make his. Then she stuck another bit onto his face to give him a beard. Actually he looked quite good.

Nadia said later that we had to call him d'Artagnan, but I don't think d'Artagnan had a beard. She said he was in disguise to fight against the Cardinal, who was just like Hitler.

Mama said the Cardinal wasn't *that* bad. Papa just stayed worried the whole day long.

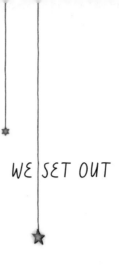

WE SET OUT

I'd forgotten to ask what time the circus began, so, to be sure not to be late, we set out just after all the churches closed their doors, when the Masses were finished.

Mama did her best and stuck some pieces of bread together with tomato paste to bring along in her bag. "It's getting to be spring," she said. "We can eat outside and then we won't look stupid if we're too early after all."

Papa was *wrong* to be so gloomy because it was a lovely day, not even one bit cold. We walked the same way as before. We didn't go the river way, which is nicer, because there were just too many stinky German trucks speeding along. They're the only ones who are allowed to drive on Sundays. That's another of their stupid laws.

This time most of the vans at the fair had their doors open. Everything looked busy. We could hear a hurdy-gurdy playing as we crossed the street and got near. There were jugglers, and stalls selling paper hats and strings of paper flowers.

"They're for men to give to their lady-loves," said Nadia. "Especially if it's their birthday."

Papa bought a pink flower for her and a white one for Mama.

There was a man walking around with a tray full of wind-up toys but they looked a bit old. There were people dressed as clowns, with white faces and hair made of mops, but they were children, really, I think, or else they may have been dwarves. There was a really great smell of burnt sausages, the kind I like best, but we couldn't see any for sale.

Nadia grabbed my arm and said, "Is that them?" And guess what, she was right.

The Corrados' van was the only yellow one. All the others were dark green or black or just plain rusty. They had made a special area in front of their van by putting sandbags in a big semi-circle. It looked like a garden, or the outside of a restaurant.

The sandbags looked like army sandbags but I don't suppose Signor Corrado had stolen them from the Germans because that would be just plain stupid. Maybe he took them from Notre-Dame Cathedral, which has lots of them outside. Anyway, the bags all had letters painted on and they spelled out the words MAGIC GARDEN. There was a flag stuck to the door of the caravan that said CORRADO FAMILY CIRCUS – NO. 1 IN EUROPE.

Once you stepped over the sandbags there were five rows of wooden seats. Four of the seats in the front row had paper signs that said RESERVED. I couldn't believe they were for us but they were, because Signor Corrado stepped out of the van right that minute and when he saw me he clapped his hands and called us all over. He bowed and pointed towards the seats. He made a special fuss over Mama and kissed her hand.

Papa looked embarrassed. "We'll stand over there," he said. He pointed towards the row of trees. "But the children can sit, thank you."

Signor Corrado wiggled his eyebrows like a clown but Papa shook his head. "It would be best for everybody if we did that," he said. "But thank you, again."

Mama looked a bit sad about the seats but then she kissed us and pushed us forward. "Enjoy the show!" she said. "We'll just walk about. Forget about us, we'll be fine."

Then I saw La Giaconda standing in the door-way of the caravan. She was wearing a black dress made of net and her long curly hair was loose over her shoulders. She gave me a big wave.

"Welcome, Jonas!" she called. "You're in for a treat today."

I made Nadia sit down in the front row and then I went over to La Giaconda to tell her it was my sister's birthday. Well, why not?

THE SHOW

The seats filled up pretty quickly but Nadia and I definitely had the best ones. She was breathing fast, as if she'd been running, she was so excited.

I kept looking round to make sure there were no soldiers hanging around. They can go to anything they want to in Paris. Which isn't fair because they have special free cinemas of their own, and eating places just for them where they can get all kinds of food. Even steaks. But there weren't any soldiers there.

There were a couple of policemen patrolling the street behind the vans, but they didn't come over. They'd probably seen the show a few times.

Signor Corrado set up a wire between two poles.

Then he began to fit a lot of stripy poles together, one into another, so it made a really long pole. It looked even longer than the ones knights used to joust with from their horses.

When the pole was ready La Giaconda came out of the van holding a little accordion. She played a really sad song, just a few bars. Signor Corrado looked as if he was crying but that was because he had tears painted under his eyes. He was wearing the same Pierrot costume as he had on the day I saw him first.

Then she began a fast funny tune, and before we could even see him do it Signor Corrado had bounced up onto the wire and was walking on it, holding the long pole. It reached nearly as far as our seats.

First he walked, and then he ran because the music was getting faster and faster. In the end he was really sliding across, as if the wire was the skinniest piece of ice ever. Then he did the splits on it. Ouch!

We all clapped when he jumped down and rolled over in a somersault.

He bowed and said, "Welcome," to everybody.

"One day, my good friends, my family will have our Big Top again and when you come you'll see me and all the other artists working with a proper trapeze and a proper high wire, just like in the old days." He pretended to wipe away his tears.

Then La Giaconda sat down in a velvet armchair. She said that she was La Giaconda, the muse of the great artist Leonardo da Vinci. Signor Corrado signalled for all of us to clap.

"I have special powers given to me by direct line from none other than the lovely Mona Lisa herself," she said. "La Giaconda. Another Italian guest living in your beautiful city."

"Not any more, she's not!" someone shouted. "She's run away, like you!"

La Giaconda got pink in her cheeks.

"Good French people are keeping her safe," she said. "Thank you."

Some people at the back began to laugh so I turned round and glared but they probably didn't see me. Anyway, they stopped when La Giaconda said she could read people's minds. She wagged her finger like a teacher.

"So all of you should be very careful what you're thinking!"

And then, before I could see it coming, she pointed at Nadia and called her over. She patted her lap as if that was where Nadia should sit.

She said, "I'm going to test my powers on this lovely young girl. I swear to you I have never set eyes on her before this day."

That was true, I knew, but still, I'd just told her

about Nadia's birthday. I really, *really* didn't want La Giaconda to make my sister look silly in any way. Don't forget, Nadia is deaf. And she can be shy with new people.

But guess what, Nadia didn't mind! She just sprang out of her seat. I looked round to see if Mama and Papa were watching. I couldn't see them but it was too late to do anything about it. There was my sister, right up there, sitting on La Giaconda's lap.

La Giaconda put her hands on Nadia's head.

"This is a very talented young lady," she said. "Artistic too. I'll bet she runs a theatrical establishment of her very own. Isn't that right?"

I nearly whooped out loud. How could La Giaconda know about Nadia's theatre? I hadn't said anything about *that*.

But there was a problem. Nadia wasn't facing La Giaconda, so she wasn't able to read her lips. She probably didn't even know there'd been a question. And she wasn't looking at me, making mad signs at her to look behind.

Then something amazing happened. Nadia turned round and said to La Giaconda, "Will you say that again, please? I didn't catch what you said."

My sister was so smart! She'd said just the right

thing, so La Giaconda asked her question about the theatre again.

Nadia blushed red. "Yes, I've got a puppet theatre, with kings and queens and a Puss in Boots."

She forgot to say d'Artagnan.

Then La Giaconda said, "But you don't have this one."

She opened her hand. Everybody except those in the front row had to stretch their necks to see what she had in it. We could see it really well. It was a tiny wooden puppet, a marionette with yellow strings, wearing a beautiful Pierrot costume. It looked exactly like Signor Corrado.

La Giaconda made it walk in the air and do the splits just like him.

"This is for you, Nadia," she said. She looked at the audience, row by row. "My muse, the famous lady in the painting, has just let me know that today is your birthday and you are eight years of age."

That was another weird thing. I hadn't told La Giaconda Nadia's age so I don't know how she got *that* right, as Nadia is so small. But she did.

One girl behind us started to cry, I suppose she was jealous about the puppet, but everybody else clapped and cheered. Then Signor Corrado made everybody sing "Happy Birthday" and he bowed Nadia back into her seat, clapping away himself.

Her face was bright pink but really happy, you could see that, and she had the puppet held tight in her hands.

I was a bit jealous too, but I knew that puppet was the best present Nadia would ever get in her whole entire life.

THE REST OF THE SHOW

"Now put your hands together for Madame Fifi and her canny canines!"

Signor Corrado started the clapping again.

Madame Fifi came out of the yellow van. She bowed. She had a set of red buckets held up against her chest and a big silver hoop looped around her neck. She was small and fat but you should have heard the whistle she made. Even Georges Leclercq couldn't do better, and he was the best whistler in our school.

The old woman sitting beside me started to shake when the poodles came out after the whistle and began to do their tricks. She was trying not to laugh but that was impossible because the dogs kept falling off the buckets. Or else they pushed them over and stuck their heads inside. One wore his bucket like a hat and he kept bumping into the others because he couldn't see. Only one of the dogs made it through the hoop properly. The others just stuck their heads through it and shook themselves and turned away as if they were saying, "Thanks but no thanks." Everyone was laughing at them. I looked towards the trees again and this time I saw Papa. He was laughing too!

Afterwards I found out that Madame Fifi's dogs were really clown dogs. They were supposed to make us laugh, not do everything right. But one thing they were all really good at was walking on their hind legs. That reminded me of Jean-Paul's dog, Whistle, and I wondered where he was. Somewhere in France, I suppose. Unless the Germans carried him off back to Germany to give to Hitler as a spoil of war.

Then Signor Corrado came back. He said he had a special treat but people would have to make a proper queue like a shop queue and come up close, one at a time, to see it.

"Because, ladies and gentlemen, this is a very tiny piece of genuine magic."

Everyone groaned but they weren't cross, not really, you could tell. Signor Corrado pointed at me.

"I'll need my young friend from the front row. He can act as my adjutant."

I didn't know what that meant but later I found out Signor Corrado liked to use strange words when he was performing. Adjutant means a kind of helper.

Anyway, *that* is how I got to see the best part of the show really close up, and for all the time it lasted, not like everybody else who had only a minute or so to look.

THE VERY, VERY SMALL CIRCUS
OF LUIGI CORRADO

Signor Corrado went back into the van and brought out a tiny theatre. It wasn't like Nadia's, it was more like the puppet theatre in the Luxembourg Gardens, because it had legs. Only it was much smaller and not as brightly painted. The top came up as high as his chest.

Then he brought out a yellow suitcase with labels stuck all over it. They said MOSCOW and VIENNA and COPENHAGEN and ROME and some other places.

He gave the suitcase to me and said really loudly, "On no account open those clasps, young man. I'm not responsible for what happens if you do."

I had no idea what was in the case but it was very, *very* light. I thought it might be full of small balloons that would float off. Or flat ones I'd have to blow up. Or else maybe stink bombs that might explode when they felt the air.

But it wasn't any of those.

When he had the theatre set up right with its little platform sticking out in front, Signor Corrado told me to put the suitcase down on the platform, facing out to the audience.

"Do *not* go near the clasps!" he said. "Only I, Luigi Corrado, can deal with the menace that lurks inside this case."

I could hear people whispering down in the rows of chairs. Someone shouted that he was itchy already, but everyone else shushed him.

Then La Giaconda appeared from behind the caravan with a long wooden flute and began to play the strangest tune you ever heard. It was as if she was calling something out of a magic forest. I'd never heard a sound like it before. As she played, the lid of the suitcase began to rise, even though Signor Corrado was standing well away and had his hands down by his sides.

I could see everything because I was so close.

The lid went up. It was lined with golden shiny material and so was the bottom part, which was raised level with the rim of the suitcase. There were four tiny Roman chariots lined up at one end.

A wall divided the middle of the ring but there was space at both ends. The wall had ancient Romans painted onto it, some in togas, some with helmets. I think it was meant to be the Colosseum.

Two of the chariots were shifting a bit as if they wanted to start racing but I couldn't figure out how they were doing it. Nobody was touching anything and there were no wires that I could see.

Then Signor Corrado pointed to the people in the front row and told them to come up. When they got close he moved forward and tapped underneath the platform. All the chariots took off! One of them got right ahead and went round the middle at a lick but then it bumped itself over and was passed by the others.

I kept looking at the crashed one because right away I could see the tiny, tiny legs. There really was something pulling the chariots along!

It was a real live flea circus. I'd read about them in my comics.

La Giaconda stopped playing. She came forward and used her flute to move people into two lines and after they'd had their look at the chariots racing she pointed them back to their seats. Mostly they said nothing much. One boy asked if he could hold one of the chariots on his arm like he did last year but Signor Corrado smiled and shook his head.

The man who'd said he was itchy started scratching really hard when he came up. It was the fifth time the chariots were going round. I knew the man was just stupid but it was making me itchy just to see him scratch. He had pimply skin all over his arms.

But Signor Corrado was able to deal with him. He spoke in a very loud voice so everybody could hear. He said the man should show some respect for the rare art of the flea circus.

"Because, ladies and gentlemen, these tiny patriotic French animals are straining their hearts and their extraordinary leg muscles to give pleasure in a grey and cold world."

I remember his words perfectly. Because it was right then that I decided I would have a flea circus of my own. Anyone could get fleas. They weren't rare, like lions. I just needed to learn how to train them. When I got good at it I'd be able to earn a bit of money and we could buy some nice things on the black market. Then Papa wouldn't have to sell any more watches.

TROUBLE

The show was nearly finished. Signor Corrado lowered the lid of the suitcase and told me I could sit down. La Giaconda came out of the caravan holding a cowboy's hat and started to go between the lines, collecting money.

The last act was Alfredo. He slinked out of the van wearing a kind of ballet costume for men. He was Signor Corrado's nephew, but this was the first time I'd seen him. He was very thin, especially his face and his legs, but he had as much hair on his head as a lion, except it was greased back.

He juggled with balls and then with some pretend swords, and Signor Corrado played the organ. Every time Alfredo dropped something Signor

Corrado played a bad chord. It was clever because people didn't know whether to boo or not. They thought maybe Alfredo was a clown, like the poodles.

But in the end some of them booed anyway. Then the noise behind us got really loud. The man who'd been causing the flea trouble stood up and pointed at where Mama and Papa were, under the trees. He shouted out, really loud.

"What about them, over there? Why do the likes of them get to stand there and look for free when we have to pay? Don't tell me *they're* patriotic Frenchmen! We know what they are!"

Everybody looked. You should have seen Mama's face. She looked as if she would faint. Papa took her hand and led her off, away from us. But they kept their heads high, at least as long as I could keep them in view. Signor Corrado made a face at me that meant stay right where you are. Nadia put her hand in mine, the one that was still holding the marionette. The poor old marionette was shaking like a skeleton.

Some people began to call out to the man, "Shame" and "Steady on", things like that. But he was still shouting after Mama and Papa.

"See how they run! See how they run!"

One of his friends roared out a horrible word.

I won't write it down. I hoped Mama was too far away to hear it.

But you'll never guess what happened next. One of the policemen on street patrol rushed over and stood right in front of the line that was making all the noise. He held up his big stick and made sure they all saw it. Then, in a loud voice, he told the man to leave.

"Get out now, thug. But not before you put some money in the lady's hat. And if I ever see you here again, ruining everyone's fun, I'll lock you up in a heartbeat."

La Giaconda spoke loudly too. She said, "We don't want money from the likes of him, Officer. But thank you for your help."

The man had to get up and go off, all red in the face, and his line of friends too, grumbling away. Everyone else watched. Someone cheered and someone booed.

But when the man got as far as the road he turned round and roared back at us.

"It won't be long now till this country is cleaned up! We'll see who gets kicked out then!"

The policeman shook his stick at him again and began to move after him, and the man ran off.

Signor Corrado came over and stood in front of Nadia and me.

"Don't worry, my brave ones," he said. "Alfredo is already on his way to fetch your parents. They won't have gone far. You just sit tight and when they come back I have something to ask them."

TOMMASO'S EARS

It didn't take long. We saw Alfredo coming back, leading Mama and Papa. He looked like a skinny sausage bobbing along in front of them. Or like the stripy Pied Piper that Mama had told us about.

Everyone else had left.

Nadia rushed towards Mama and hugged her. Signor Corrado held out his hand and helped them step over the sandbags. "I apologize sincerely," he said. "Nothing like that has ever happened before at any performance of ours."

Mama had tears in her eyes but Papa was boiling inside. I could see that.

"You see what they've made of our country?" he said. "Of course, it's not your fault, Signor. But we can't breathe the air itself now, it seems."

Signor Corrado told us all to sit down.

"I have a proposal," he said. "I know it will sound strange after all that but hear me out. My wife is joining us."

La Gioconda came down the steps of the van, leading a boy by the hand. He was about my age and he had thick black curly hair like hers. He looked pretty miserable even though he was wearing a pair of *real* football boots. They were black and gleaming with polish, as if they'd never been used.

The two of them came and stood beside Signor Corrado.

"How's my boy?" he said. "Better?" He got his fingers stuck, rubbing the boy's hair. But the boy didn't laugh. He just stood there.

"This is our Tommaso," Signor Corrado said to us. "He hasn't been at all well lately. He's been in hospital."

"Oh dear," said Mama. "Why?"

"The Necker Hospital for Sick Children," said La Gioconda. "He has a problem with his ears. Mastoid infections. He has to go back into hospital again soon."

Mama turned pink. "That's where our Nadia goes too, with her ears! Say hello to Tommaso, Nadia!"

Nadia made a face at the boy. A nice face, not a rude one. He just stared back at her and dug his boots into the ground.

"You see, Tommaso can't go to school right now," Signor Corrado said. "If you could spare your Jonas to come and help us out on Sundays and be a friend to Tommaso, I would promise to take the best care of him. Myself or Alfredo would pick him up and return him to you. We'd feed him well. And he would have absolute protection at all times."

He rubbed my hair this time. "Your Jonas is such a smart boy. He gets completely involved, a quality I like. I think he'd enjoy being part of our show. What do you think?"

What did *I* think? Take a guess! But of course it was Mama and Papa he was talking to, not me. And guess which one of them thought it was a good idea and which one a bad idea?

I bet everyone gets that one wrong.

But it wasn't decided right there on the spot, not with Tommaso ruining his boots, kicking the studs into the ground. And Papa still boiling over with fury.

Mama said, "We'd better go home and talk about this, Signor…" and she stopped.

"Corrado," said Signor Corrado. "I am Luigi and my wife is Lucia. We're from Bologna. In better times."

Then he winked at me. "Don't forget, Jonas would earn a little bit, too. The labourer is worthy of his hire."

We went home then.

But in case anybody wonders, it was Papa who thought it would be a good idea for me to come to the circus on Sundays. That was because he was all wound up and angry about the stupid laws for Jews that kept us down. He didn't think the horrible man at the circus would make any bother for me, because he hadn't even noticed me.

But Mama was just plain scared about it all.

"You said he should have other boys to play with," Papa said. "I don't want him at school, so here's his chance. And he won't be on his own, going there or coming back. He'll be with an Italian. That's a lot safer than he'd be with me."

He laughed, but it wasn't a jokey laugh. After a while Mama said she would let me go once and see how it went.

"I did like that man," she said slowly. "And I'm sorry for the poor boy. He looked so sick and unhappy."

Anyway, that's how it all began a few months ago, with me and the Corrado family. And now I am going to bed.

1 OCTOBER 1942

Today the Prof gave me my first piano lesson! He said his secret plan was moving along, little by little, but he could see it wasn't very healthy for me to be up in the attic on my own all day, even if I was devouring books.

"We'll try a lesson, Jonas. It's taken me this long to realize that even if the neighbours hear you play a few scales, they'll just think I'm taking on pupils again. Doing some work after all this time."

I suppose he meant after his wife's death.

He said he had one good neighbour who never complained about his pupils' playing and one bad neighbour who did.

"That fellow used to act as if he was under siege

by Napoléon every time the piano lid went up. The letters I used to get! Well, his holiday is over now. I'm back at my work again."

The music room was small and painted the same red cabbage colour as the hall. All that was in it was a piano, and two stools. But it was a grand piano, not an ordinary one like ours. It nearly touched the two ends of the room. It was golden-coloured and polished and the lid was open. You could see all the red hammers and the wire strings inside.

The Prof sat me down on the music stool and spun it round to make it go higher. That was fun but when it was set right he said, "Let's hear my best pupil's pupil play, then."

That made me nervous because it was so long since I'd played. And I'd *never* played a grand piano. I tried to delay by telling the Prof about playing the organ at the circus but he only laughed. He said an organ in a circus was probably specially tuned to sound ridiculous.

"After all, people expect to hear *poop-poop* noises at a circus. Don't worry, all your good work with your mother will come back to you soon enough."

Unfortunately, that wasn't true. My fingers felt as if they were just stiff bones. They wouldn't do anything I wanted them to. My scales sounded terrible, like cats walking up and down the keys.

Not even cats *running*. I wanted to say sorry to the golden piano.

The Prof told me to take a break. He played the Brahms lullaby for me and I watched his fingers.

Then he said, "Try that, Jonas. Just pick it out as you hear it in your head and don't worry about what old Herr Brahms wrote down on his music sheet."

I was much better doing that, playing by ear. I even made up something for my left hand to play, to go with the melody. It sounded all right, though I bet Brahms wouldn't have thought much of it.

We went back to doing scales and I was better that time, and then we did some Beethoven. The Prof played part of the *Moonlight Sonata* and I closed my eyes to hear it better. It was like having Mama playing in the parlour in rue de la Harpe at night, when we were in our beds.

He told me Mama was only fourteen when she became his pupil and that she'd already won lots of prizes. He said the other students called her "the lovely Berlioz", even the girls, because she was so pretty and so nice to everyone. That was a little strange, thinking about Mama at that age, only four years older than me. She married Papa when she was twenty.

Then at last I remembered to ask the Prof the

date. I was a bit surprised when he told me it was 1 October. I've got a bit confused. I think it's from being inside all the time.

Anyway, that means I've been here nearly six weeks.

I didn't tell him about my birthday. But it is exactly two weeks away. I suppose that even if I hadn't asked the date I should have guessed it by looking at the trees I can see from my room. The ones in the park, with their few leaves hanging on tight. Every year there are some leaves left when 15 October comes round. Mama says they hang around just for my birthday. But mostly, they're gone.

I can see the fallen leaves now from the attic window. They're just blowing around the paths and getting into piles in the gutters. Nobody's sweeping them or clearing them up.

The days went by so fast because I spent so much time writing about us all going to the Corrado circus. Which is odd because that was just *one* day nearly seven months ago.

But it was good to think about Nadia's birthday again. When we all meet up I'll read those chapters out to her. I think they make a good story. It's all true *and* it has a beginning, a middle and an end.

I hope she put the marionette in a safe place. She used to take it everywhere with her.

4 OCTOBER 1942

NEW CLOTHES

★

My shorts and shirt have got pretty dirty. Smelly, really. All this time the Prof has been washing my vest and underpants himself because he didn't want the laundry woman who collects his clothes to see them and start asking questions.

"There's always the possibility Madame Belcher might be a crow," he said. "With her, I'm afraid I wouldn't rule it out."

He told me crows are people who write letters to the Germans telling tales on other people. They don't sign their names. They just have black hearts through and through, the colour of a crow. Now I know it must have been a crow who told the Germans about us being Jews and having a nice shop in rue de la Harpe.

There was only cold water and rough red soap to do the washing with but the Prof did his best. I said I'd do it but that was before he let me come downstairs, so I couldn't, really.

The underwear takes a long time to dry because he can't hang it out in case someone sees it. He has to hang it up in the kitchen. So when it's down there all I have to wear is the shirt and the shorts. It's getting pretty cold now and I'm going to need a jumper or two for the winter. Or else I will turn into an iceberg.

I told the Prof that La Giaconda would be sure to give me some of Tommaso's clothes, if he was to go and see her. But he said he'd see about it in his own way.

Anyway, today when he got in from the Conservatoire he came upstairs and asked me to come down to the kitchen. It was really warm there compared to my room. He had a big grin on his face. *That* was unusual. There was a brown paper parcel on the table.

"A present for you, Jonas," he said.

I didn't expect it would be anything much, but it was a proper boy's suit made of some brown woolly stuff. The suit pants were shorts, not longs, but it wasn't bad at all.

Plus there were two white shirts and new under-pants, two pairs.

I went into the piano room and put the suit on. The pants were a little scratchy on my knees where the lining ended but it was better than having smelly ones. All the Prof would tell me was that he'd made a decent swap. He didn't say what he'd swapped but I think these clothes are pretty good ones.

He said he thought that there were some warm jumpers somewhere in the house, ones that his son Robert used to wear when he was young.

"They'll be in a drawer somewhere, under moth-balls," he said. "My wife spent such a long time knit-ting them she said she'd never throw them out."

Then he looked sad so I told him the suit was the best clothes I'd had for a long time.

"My mother would love to see all these things. She'd write a letter to thank you."

I said we'd pay him back but he said not to worry about that right now. Then we had some porridge with some of the honeycomb a friend had given him and I decided to tell him about my flea circus to get him cheered up again. I'll write down pretty much what I told him.

SUNDAY AFTERNOONS
AT THE FAIR

When Papa said it was all right for me to go to the fair I started helping the Corrados every Sunday.

Well, nearly every Sunday. There was the time Nadia and I got the measles. I was much sicker than she was. Mama thought at first I must have picked it up at the circus but Giselle Bauer had the spots too and so did all the Kamynski girls on the first floor, so it was really their fault.

Papa had to sell another watch to pay for a doctor to come and see us. I don't even remember the doctor. Mama said that was because of the fever. I nearly boiled over.

All the other Sundays I went to the fairground. Usually Alfredo called for me, but sometimes it was Signor Corrado. They both knew the quickest way to Nation but Alfredo walked so fast I couldn't keep up with him. Just as well Mama didn't know *that*, what with all the potato bug patrols going past with their guns and their mean faces.

One morning when I was trailing way behind Alfredo a soldier smiled at me and pretended he was ringing a handbell. I knew straight off he thought I was a proper Catholic altar boy like Jean-Paul, even though I didn't have the dress he had. One time long ago Jean-Paul stole the handbell from his church and we played with it until Mama found out and made him take it back. Anyway, I made a really good-boy face right back to the German. Fooled him!

Most of the work I did Alfredo could have done, but he was lazy. I helped put out the chairs and arrange the sandbags and hang the flags up. La Giaconda told me that when I went around with the hat at the end of the show I got a lot more money than Alfredo did.

He didn't care, he was so lazy. Anyway, he was in love with Violette, the woman who sold cigarettes at the kiosk up the road, the one the Germans used.

Violette had a lot of hair too.

Tommaso was out of hospital on the second

Sunday I went. He was better again, they said, but I could see he was maybe a bit deaf. I knew that because of Nadia but I didn't say it to anyone else in case they worried. I didn't say it to *him* either but I taught him some of the signs we used at home with Nadia. I pretended it was a code. Which it is, really.

Tommaso wasn't Jean-Paul, but he was all right when you got to know him. He was so glad to be home again he didn't even mind me helping his parents out with the circus. What he really loved was football, so we usually kicked a ball around when everyone had gone home. Sometimes boys from the other vans came along and played too and it felt nearly like being in my schoolyard again. That was fun. We used the sandbags for goal posts.

Tommaso made us all play Italian teams. He knows every team there is, even the French teams, but we weren't allowed to be French. His favourite footballer is Giuseppe Meazza. Even *I'd* heard of him. His nickname is Peppino and he's on lots of cigarette cards. He played right here in Paris when Italy won the World Cup a few years ago.

Jean-Paul went to see the final with his father but Papa wouldn't take me. No. 1 – he said I was too small and No. 2 – he said there would be a bad lot over from Italy he didn't want to tangle with.

He didn't say No. 3, of course, which was that he didn't care anything about football. But I didn't say that to Tommaso. He definitely wouldn't understand because football is all he cares about.

La Giaconda always made a big pot of spaghetti or noodles before I went home. She just used tomato paste like the stuff in tins Mama bought, with no meat or anything like that, but hers tasted different. She said it was because the tomatoes were Italian and so were the herbs. When she couldn't find noodles she made something out of potatoes. I don't know what it was, but I could have eaten two plates of it at a time.

I always helped with the flea circus, just like the first time. And when Signor Corrado took the organ out of its tent, I always played it for Alfredo's act and for Madame Fifi and her poodles.

But one Sunday it rained and nobody came. *Nobody.* So, that day, I asked Signor Corrado if I could learn to train fleas for myself.

TA-DA!

THE AMAZING FLEA CIRCUS
OF JONAS ALBER

Signor Corrado gave me some of his special fleas to start off with. First he explained that all a flea wants to do in its whole life is jump. Except when it's biting you and drinking your blood.

If our legs had the strength of a flea's legs we would be able to jump as high as the moon. Well, pretty high, anyway. Definitely as high as the Eiffel Tower. Maybe as high as Mount Everest, which is the highest mountain in the world. Nobody has ever climbed to the top of it. Or if they did, they didn't come back alive.

Here is something most people don't know: there are mountains that are even higher than Everest. They're in the oceans. The basking sharks swim over them all the time. So do ships, and that's why some ships disappear. If they strike the top of an underwater mountain they sink to the bottom of the ocean and nobody ever finds them.

Anyway, if you harness a flea to something like a chariot it will pull it along because it wants to jump. It can't jump so it pulls the chariot instead, even though the chariot is much bigger than the flea. Signor Corrado said this is flea power at work.

Some people think flea circuses are all a trick of the eye but they are not. At least mine wasn't, and Signor Corrado's wasn't.

You need neat fingers and ladies' tweezers or the fleas will get away. It's tricky. I lost a few before I learned how to lift them properly from the box and harness them and then put them back in the box again afterwards. I hope the ones that got away jumped right on top of a fat potato bug and sucked out lots of his blood.

Mama wasn't one bit happy about me training fleas. The first day I came home with the box of fleas and the chariots that Signor Corrado had given me, she screamed and ran out onto the landing.

Papa was interested, though, when I told him about the leg muscles fleas have. He took a good hard look at the cardboard chariots when I had everything working and he said he was sure he could make something better for me.

He was doing a few jobs by then but because that was against the law for Jews it had to be a secret. On Mondays and Wednesdays he went off to work with another jeweller on the Île Saint-Louis. That's quite close to rue des Lions but it's full of rich people's houses and rich people's shops.

I don't know what the other jeweller's name was. Papa wouldn't tell us. I think all Papa did was fix watches somewhere in a backyard but at least he got a little money. And he had a place to go to so he wasn't hanging around with his black face on. That's what Mama said to him one day when they had a fight. Which was awful because they never used to fight.

When he brought home the silver carriages I didn't know what to say to him. There were three carriages and each one could fit perfectly into a hazelnut shell. Papa had a shell ready, just to prove it. He had beaten the silver so fine it was thinner than paper.

Each carriage was different. One had a roof, one was open – Nadia said that one was the queen's carriage – and one was quite like a Roman chariot because it had only two wheels, not four like the others.

Papa showed me where he had stamped the hallmarks. It was done really neatly, right across the wheel axles. Hallmarks are like a code, or a signature, for things made of silver or gold. They tell you who made the piece, when it was made and where, and how much precious metal is in it.

Papa had used up some really precious silver to make my flea carriages. That made Mama very cross. For ages she wouldn't speak to him or me all evening and Nadia had to make up a spy message to tell us there was soup left out on the table for our dinner. But Papa said there was nobody left in the city who would give him a decent price for the silver.

"Why shouldn't the boy have some fun, anyway?" he said. "And if they raid our house, or if anything happens to us, that bit of silver will stay out of German hands as long as Jonas keeps it with his friends. That's worth something, surely?"

Papa had begun to say things like that. He said the mood was turning nastier by the day, even though the winter was over. Mama had those lines around her mouth all the time now, even when Papa was safe at home. She didn't tell us stories anymore. She just told us what we should do if something happened to Papa and her, and we were left on our own.

She told me I should take Nadia and go straight to the old church behind rue de la Harpe and tell the priest there who we were.

"He's duty-bound to help you," she said.

I didn't think so. Surely Monsieur Zacharides would be better because he was our friend? But she shook her head and made me promise to do what she said.

But she let me go to the circus every Sunday, even though Papa had wasted the silver, and even though Tommaso was getting better. She told me it was really because of the noodles.

"I think you're growing a bit, Jonas, with that extra meal Signora Corrado gives you, whatever she puts into it," she said. "And Nadia can eat your share here so it suits all of us."

Poor Mama. She did her best but she felt worse and worse. I could hear her crying at night sometimes, though I never told Nadia that. Sometimes I felt glad to be away from our apartment and with the Corrados, but I couldn't tell anybody that. So, in the end I felt bad about *that* too.

But every Sunday I got better at the work. Signor Corrado let me use his theatre to show off my fleas and La Giaconda found a piece of black velvet which showed the silver carriages off really well.

What I liked best was having the carriages on

my arm, making the fleas pull them from my elbow to my wrist. Their legs tickled! When people saw that they wanted to do it too so I charged them for it and Signor Corrado let me keep that money. Girls and women *never* wanted to do it but they always looked at the men who did. Sometimes they screamed.

I called my fleas Athos, Porthos and Aramis because they were the Three Musketeers. To be honest, I didn't really know which one was which and there were always lots more than three fleas in the box anyway.

At the circus you have to pretend a lot. I told people Athos was the clever one, Porthos was the fat one and Aramis was the joker. They laughed. People like you to tell them stuff like that, especially if you mix the facts up a bit. It becomes a new kind of a story and people like to hear stories, even when there is a war on.

Especially when there's a war on, La Giaconda said.

Last night I dreamed that Jean-Paul came to the circus. He had Whistle with him and we put on our own circus, just the two of us, me with my fleas and him with his dog. Only it was in a railway station, not out in the open air at Nation. All the trains waited until our show was finished and then they all took off at the same time, tearing down the tracks as if they were in a race. They made loads of steam and when it was all gone so was Jean-Paul.

I really missed him.

THE KNOCK AT THE DOOR

The Prof lets me come down to the kitchen now for all our meals. When he goes out I'm supposed to go back upstairs and stay there, in case I drop something and the neighbours hear the noise. He told me that patrols were beginning to call at houses for no reason, even in a street like this one where no Jews are living any more. Apparently, before I came here somebody's house down the street had been cleared out, just like our shop. The Prof looked really sad when he told me that.

But when he headed out today I knew he wouldn't be long so I decided to stay in the kitchen. It's really cold at the top of the house. Anyway, he'd only gone to the rue Mouffetard, which is close by. He said if there was any street in Paris where there'd be cheese for sale that'd be the one.

He told me one day he'd seen a shop window with beautiful cheeses on plates and there was no queue outside, but when he got up close there was a sign under the cheese that said "Everything here is false". He said he laughed so much it was nearly better than real cheese. Try telling that to a mouse, though.

Anyway, I washed up our porridge bowls and then I sat down to read. I was still at the Atlantic Ocean in the A–L encyclopedia. I've never seen any ocean in all my life but that's the one I want to see most. It has the basking sharks, of course, but also lots of different whales. It stretches all the way down from the Arctic Ocean to the Antarctic Ocean.

The eels are in the middle, close to America. Eels have their own part of the ocean which is called the Sargasso Sea. Every eel in Europe and America has to go there to breed. Then they die, which isn't really fair after going all that long distance. But the clever thing is that their children come back to the country their parents came from. It takes them years but they have a good system and they just know how to do it. They never make mistakes, unless they get eaten by a shark or a big fish or get caught in a fishing net.

I was drawing a picture of the Sargasso Sea, filling

it with eels of all different sizes. Then – CRASH!
BANG! – there was the worst noise you ever heard
at the front door.

It was much worse than knocking. It was hammering and banging. Someone began to shout. I couldn't make out the words so I was sure they must be German. Whoever it was sounded really, *really* angry. The banging just got louder and then something made of metal started to make a cruel hurting noise against the door. They were going to splinter it to bits.

I knew right that minute that it must have been like this for Mama and Papa that morning in July. What did they do? Did they open the door or did they let it be broken down? Which was worse? Did Mama try to hide Nadia under the bed, telling her to run to the church on her own afterwards?

I couldn't run anywhere now. If I tried to go upstairs they'd see me through the smashed door. But if I waited they'd be in the hall in a minute. The kitchen was only a couple of steps down from the hall and then they'd find me.

And I couldn't just open the door now, not after all the banging.

"Who are you? Why didn't you open up straightaway? Where are your papers? Don't you know we're cleaning up this country?"

That's what they'd shout at me when they saw me.

But first they shouted something else.

"OPEN UP, BY ORDER OF THE—"

I didn't catch the next word, but now I could make out that they were speaking French. And then someone swore and a dog barked.

Everyone knew the Germans had search dogs. They could sniff people out, even if they were covered in meat and hiding in a butcher's shop.

HIDING

The window in the kitchen was very small and very high up. There was a tiny yard outside but the Prof had told me that if you went out there you could be seen from the other houses. And there was no kitchen cupboard deep enough for me to fit into and hide, because they all had narrow rows of shelves inside them. Anyway, you can bet Germans know full well to throw open the cupboards first thing when they break into a house.

But the kitchen was the only place I had.

I got up really, *really* quietly and went to the cupboard nearest the cooker, where the Prof kept his sheets and towels. I rooted out some of these and then I sat on the floor and curled up. I pulled a few of the sheets and towels down and wrapped them around me, underneath as well. I wanted it to look as if the linens had fallen out while the Prof was in a mad rush looking for a clean shirt, or something. But I knew it wouldn't fool the dog.

Then I just sat. If I put my hands over my ears it would block out the noise at the door, but it would be worse not to know what was happening. Suppose they got in and I missed hearing that and then I sneezed? So I waited.

Maybe it wasn't even me they were after. Maybe the Prof had done something else wrong. Maybe he was a Commie. Papa said the Germans hated Commies nearly as much as they hated Jews. That's because they're fighting the Russians now and they're Commies.

If the police came and took the Prof away what would I do? What would he do? He was so old.

I was breathing so fast I was sucking the sheet into my mouth. I'd no spit left and I really wanted to cough. Then I heard the door being flung open. Boots in the hall. It sounded like there was a whole battalion out there.

I peed a little then, because of the shock, but I managed to stop. I tried to make myself stop shaking too. Towels don't shake. I tried to breathe through my nose. Then I tried to become invisible.

Signor Corrado says if you do a trick you have to believe in it yourself, totally.

"Do you know why everybody believes my wife looks just like the Mona Lisa, Jonas?" he asked me one day. "It's because she believes it herself."

He said an acrobat or a wire walker has to believe they can fly or walk through the air. They have to believe they will never fall. Or else they will.

I had to be a towel or a pillow case that nobody would even notice if they walked into the kitchen, but I didn't believe it myself. Anyone would see I was a boy. The dog would tell them. And if they had bayonets they could find out for sure.

AN EMERGENCY

Then I heard the Prof. He was in the hall too, and he was shouting above the noise of the boots tramping around.

"Who are you? How dare you break into my house!"

He sounded really brave. After all, they must have all had their guns pointed at him. And I'd never have thought he could shout like that. He sounded scary when he should have been scared, like I was.

The boots stopped right where they were, just before they'd reached the steps to the kitchen.

Then someone said, "We apologize, Monsieur. But your neighbours said you weren't home and this is an emergency. There's a bad leak on the street and that means trouble with your inflow pipe. If we don't fix it the street pipe will fail, and so will yours, and your house will be destroyed."

It was the fire brigade! Not the Germans. Not the police. And the dog that barked must have been just a normal dog walking by who didn't like all the racket.

But what could I do now? I couldn't come out because the firemen would know there was a boy in hiding, someone who didn't answer the door even when someone else was battering it down. And the poor Prof standing out there in the hall didn't even know where I was.

But he was smart. He guessed I'd stayed in the kitchen. I don't know how. That Prof was as smart as any spy.

He said, "Give me one minute to move a few things I have in the kitchen."

I didn't move, even when I heard his step. Then he was right beside me. He picked me up carefully and threw me across his shoulder and then he reached in for more sheets and put them over me so that they hung down. Then we were out in the hall and we were going up the stairs and he said, "Go right ahead, gentlemen. And thank you for allowing me to save my wife's best linen."

He brought me up to his room, set me down on the bed and lifted the sheets and towels from me. He kept one finger stuck to his lips. Not that I needed to be told *that*. Then he pointed me towards his wardrobe. I climbed into it and he piled the linens in on top of me.

"Stay brave, Jonas," he whispered. Then he was off downstairs again.

I took the sheets away from my face. I could breathe again, just about, even though there was a fur coat brushing against my face and tickling me. It was very dark in the wardrobe and there was nothing to hear.

I think I fell asleep then, which was a pretty stupid thing to do because if anyone had opened the wardrobe they'd have seen my face shining out of the dark like a moon. But I woke up when the Prof touched my shoulder and told me I could come out.

"They've gone, Jonas. They've managed to shore up the leak too. It's all right, it's just a bit damp down there. We'll take care of it after we get something to eat."

When I came out my legs were too wobbly to work properly. Jean-Paul and I used to make our legs go all shaky when we were playing soldiers and falling down on the ground and dying. But it isn't funny when it's real and you can't control it.

The Prof told me to take my time so I sat down on the bedroom floor and stretched out my legs and gave them a good bashing with my fists, the way I'd seen Signor Corrado and La Giaconda do every Sunday afternoon before the circus opened. Then my legs were all right again and I was able to walk downstairs without falling.

AND THE DATE WAS...

The Prof didn't say anything cross to me. He made us both some strong coffee. He put honey into it to make it sweet. He said if he'd had any brandy he'd have used that too, even for me.

"I wasn't able to get cheese, after all," he said. "But look – chicken livers!"

He fried the liver with some flat rissoles he'd made with leftover turnips. He says there are women in the queues who tell him how to cook things, just because he's a man. But they've got no idea what a good cook he is. I wonder if Mama knew that about him.

He'd bought a newspaper too, which he didn't usually do because he said they were rubbish. Papa said the same thing but sometimes he picked one up so we'd have something to light the fire with afterwards. Anyway, the Prof read his paper and let me eat.

The encyclopedia was where I'd left it, open at the eels. It was lucky it hadn't fallen off onto the floor because the whole room was really wet under our feet, just as bad as a street gets after it rains really hard. There were even some deep puddles. Bad tiling, the Prof said.

When he'd read his newspaper he threw sheets of it down to soak up the worst puddles. That's when I saw the date. It was 15 October. I'd forgotten to count. *Again*.

My birthday. I am ten.

I didn't say anything to the Prof because he'd get all embarrassed and start thinking he should get a cake for me, or something else that was impossible. I'd been wondering if the Corrados would get a card in the post for me, from Mama and Papa. But if they had, surely Signor Corrado would have delivered it.

I wanted a card more than anything. Because today it's exactly three months since I saw my family. And if what happened on that day hadn't happened, I'd be with them now, wherever they are. We'd all be together and they'd know it was my birthday and it wouldn't matter that there wasn't any cake or presents or stuff.

The Prof said he was going to knock at the good neighbour's door and see if there was a mop or some cloths he could borrow. Then we'd mop up the kitchen, just the two of us, and when that was done he was going to get a locksmith to come and fix the door. I'd have to go back to the attic.

So that's what we did on 15 October 1942. We cleaned up the big mess in the kitchen and then I went upstairs to my room.

Outside on the street the firemen had left some pipes lying around. I saw a delivery van from the Bon Marché store coming along, pulled by two big grey horses. When the horses saw the pipes they wouldn't go any further, even though the driver used his big whip on them. He had to climb down and pull out a hamper from the van and walk. I couldn't see which number he knocked at but it was a few houses down. The Prof must have some really rich neighbours if they get deliveries like that.

Before it got completely dark I tore out a page from this notebook and made a birthday card for myself. It didn't say anything very much because I don't know what my family is doing right now. This is all it says:

"To our beloved Jonas on the occasion of his

tenth birthday from his mama and papa, and also from his dear sister Nadia."

The first part is what our parents always put on our birthday cards. I just added Nadia this time because I didn't want her to feel left out.

On the inside I drew a cartoon of my fleas. Only instead of pulling carriages they were marching in a band. Athos had a trumpet, Porthos a big drum sitting on his fat tummy, and Aramis a triangle that had two crotchets jumping out of it. Drawing the cartoon cheered me up, though I bet Mama wouldn't have liked it as much as I did.

THIS IS WHAT HAPPENED ON 15 JULY 1942

We never had any visitors in rue des Lions. Except for Giselle Bauer, of course, and she doesn't count. Papa went out on his own if he wanted to meet someone and Mama never went out at all, except with us and Papa, or to the shops to queue for food. On Sundays Signor Corrado or Alfredo called for me and brought me home again but they never came inside.

But on the morning of 15 July, Mama came into the room where Nadia and I slept. She shook me awake.

"Hurry up, Jonas, and go downstairs. Signor Corrado is knocking at the door for you and calling out like a madman."

Signor Corrado! But I'd been helping him just

the day before. It was a Tuesday, not a Sunday, but that's because Tuesday was the 14 July holiday. There were two shows, not just one. We'd never had such a busy day. Everybody said the summer had come at last.

"People just want to come out of their sad little rooms and have some fun," said La Giaconda. "Let's pull out all the stops!"

So we did. For both shows. I made quite a bit of money with my flea circus that day.

There were only two things that weren't good. The first was that Tommaso had been tired. He said he was too tired to help me and too tired to play football. Which was really odd, for *him*.

The other was that I'd seen the pimply man again, the one who wanted to clear Mama and Papa out. He was marching up and down the pathway alongside the circus, sticking out his arm and shouting German words to anyone who looked at him. There was no policeman to get rid of him this time. But Signor Corrado said not to worry, he was just a nuisance, like a wasp. In the end he went off somewhere with his gang.

I pulled my shorts on and ran downstairs. Someone had let Signor Corrado into the hall and he was just starting up the stairs. He grabbed my hands and held them.

"Jonas, please, please will you come and help us?" he said. "Tommaso asked for you to come. He has to go back to hospital but he won't go unless you come too. He's sore in his head and he's very weak. Please go and ask your parents. But hurry."

He looked really pale, and Signor Corrado *never* looked pale. He followed me back upstairs. Mama had a pot of water on the stove for the awful coffee but he shook his head. He told Mama and Papa about Tommaso.

"It's his mastoid again," he said. "He was in terrible pain last night. Now the pain is gone and he's just weak but he wants Jonas. He says he won't go to the hospital without him."

"But surely the hospital won't let Jonas in, Signor," Mama said. I knew from the way she spoke that she didn't want me going to the Corrados' again so soon.

It was Papa who said I should go. "He doesn't have to go to the hospital at all, my dear," he said to Mama. "He only has to coax Tommaso to go. If anyone can coax a body to do something our Jonas can."

Papa said that about *me*. I could hardly believe it.

"Take my bike," he said to Signor Corrado. "Keep it. I can't use it since we've had to wear these things." He meant the yellow stars.

Mama told me to put a clean shirt on and to wash my face and hands. They both came downstairs with us. Mama wasn't a bit pleased but she hugged me like a bear, really tight. They shook hands with Signor Corrado and then we were up on the bike, me on the crossbar.

I could see the stupid Kamynski girls at the window, laughing and pointing, but I ignored them. What did they know about anything? They never even went out. I looked up but Nadia wasn't at our window. She was still in bed. She hadn't heard Mama come in. She was probably dreaming about Puss in Boots or d'Artagnan.

Signor Corrado pushed the pedals down and we began to wobble off. Then Mama suddenly gave a little cry. "Wait! Please! Just one minute!"

She ran back into the house. Poor Signor Corrado looked desperate but Mama took no time at all. She had a little flat card in her hand. "Take this," she said to me. "I meant to give you this before now. If anything goes wrong this dear man will help you."

I put the card in my pocket. I didn't even look at it. Then we started out again. And Signor Corrado rode like he had a yellow jersey on, not at all like poor Papa who had to stop all the time just to get his breath back.

TOMMASO

Tommaso was in his bunk-bed inside the van. He had a wet bandage wound round his head and for some reason a black patch over one eye. He looked exactly like Filochard from my *Pieds nickelés* comics but of course I didn't say that.

La Giaconda was holding his hands but she got up to kiss me. Then she made me stand where Tommaso could see me with his one eye, without having to move his head. She said that hurt him.

"Bambino, here's our dear Jonas come to see you," she said. "Now, you listen to him and do what he says. He's a clever boy."

Do what *I* said! That would never happen in our family. We just did what we were told. But I did my best. I told Tommaso that the hospital would fix him up just like they'd done with Nadia.

"They'll have nice food, maybe even ice cream. They want everyone to get better quickly."

I could see by the look he gave me he thought this was just a big lie. It's funny that even one eye can let you know that much. So I tried harder. I promised him all my comics, but he didn't even blink. I tried to think of everything Tommaso liked. Then I remembered the best thing. I went right over to the bed so he couldn't miss what I said.

"I'll write a letter to Peppino at his football club and tell him you're in hospital. When he writes back then you'll have his autograph and it'll be worth a fortune. But he won't write back unless you're in hospital because he'll have to feel sorry for you and he won't if you're just at home like any other boy. So you have to go to the hospital to have a proper hospital address."

La Giaconda squeezed my hand hard. "Look, Jonas," she said. "He's smiling!"

Maybe he was, but it wasn't much of a smile. Then the one eye closed.

Signor Corrado had stayed at the door. "What do you think, my love?" he asked. "Will I go for them?"

"Yes!" she said. "Go!"

And then she said to me, "You'll have to hide for a bit, Jonas. He's gone for our friend, the policeman. He promised us they'll take Tommaso to the hospital in their van. That's the best way. And it's so far away. But you'd better not be found here by the police, not without your papers."

She lifted up the big curtain with the printed stars that I'd seen the first day, the day I met the Corrados.

"In there, pet. There's room under Alfredo's bunk."

I looked back at Tommaso but he seemed to be asleep. I thought of the comics I'd promised to give him. He might not be able to read them because they were in French, not Italian, but it was too late. And now I had to find out where Peppino's club was so we could get a letter to him.

"Right," I said.

That was the first time I got under Alfredo's bunk.

NO WAY HOME

I heard the policemen coming into the van, two of them. Their boots sounded loud and mean from where I was but at least they didn't shout and bang on the door. That's what you heard them do up and down our street, whenever they saw any bit of light escaping from a window at night, or when they came looking for people's identity papers.

Tommaso didn't make any noise at all when they carried him out. He must have been properly asleep by then.

Both La Giaconda and Signor Corrado went away with him and the policemen. I fell asleep for a while and the next thing I knew, Alfredo was coming in.

It was the smell of his cigarette that woke me up. I could see his long spidery legs and his pointy shoes with the heels made of cork, like Mama's. He nearly jumped out of his skin when I whispered to him from under the bed. Then he got cross.

"Get right out here so I can see you," he said. "I'm not going to talk to someone with no face."

When I said I was just doing what La Giaconda had told me to, he got even crosser.

"Of course it's all right to come out now!" he said. "Do you think you're some great Resistance hero and the cabbage-heads are all waiting outside the van to pounce on you? Get up!"

He heated some beans for the two of us. Then Madame Fifi came in with her dogs. Every day she walks them down to the huge market at Les Halles, just before it closes, and somehow she gets enough scraps for all the dogs to eat. Tommaso told me she puts on a special show for the butchers there, the ones that wear the funny hats. She doesn't bring her buckets, though. They were in a heap in the corner of the van.

She wasn't surprised to see me and neither were the dogs. Oscar jumped up on my lap and licked me. He had horrible bad breath so the butchers must have given him something smelly to eat.

When Alfredo cleared the table Madame Fifi sat

down and started to play solitaire. I said I'd better go home.

"You can't go now," Madame Fifi said. "It's nearly curfew time. And there's something up tonight, anyway. There are police on every corner between here and the markets. *Far* more than the usual band of blackguards."

She banged down a card. "And with the kind of papers you have, Jonas, or don't have, I can never remember which it is, if they stopped you they'd just throw you over to the Boche. Maybe to the Gestapo, and they're the worst of the lot."

"Don't say that to him," Alfredo said. "He's cocky enough."

"I don't have my papers here," I said. "But I have to get home. My parents will go wild if I stay out."

"Sorry, hero," said Alfredo. "You can't go. Anyway, they'll know it's to do with Tommaso. Your parents, I mean. They'll know you're with us."

I went to the door. It wasn't completely dark outside yet because it was summer but it was very quiet. At least it was quiet until the German patrols went tramping by.

What should I do? I was a bit afraid now. Madame Fifi seemed very sure about all that police stuff. Mama wouldn't want me to do anything stupid, especially with the curfew. Suppose old

Pimply "Sieg Heil" Arms was still prowling around somewhere? I didn't even know if he knew I was Jewish and shouldn't be at the circus at all.

Alfredo was probably right. My parents would guess that something was up, something that meant I had to stay. But I really really didn't like not being with them. Me and Nadia – we'd never spent even one night away from our parents in all our lives. She always liked to sign me some daft story before we went to sleep. She'd never speak it. It was to test my signing.

These days the stories were always about d'Artagnan. Guess what, he was lonely after the other musketeers had been turned into fleas so he was sending messages to them through me. It was just like the wireless from London, only for fleas. That's how daft Nadia is.

But I waited. It got all dark in the end and then Signor Corrado and La Giaconda came. They'd had to walk back but they had a special note from the doctors in case they met a patrol.

"Did you notice all the policemen around the place, sprung up like mushrooms in the dark?" Madame Fifi asked. They hadn't. But then they were bothered about Tommaso.

"They said he was very weak," La Giaconda said. "But they have good medicine and he's in a ward with lots of other children so he'll have company."

"He'll do just fine," Signor Corrado said.

He hugged me and told me he'd take me back home on Papa's bike in the morning.

"We're ever so grateful to you for helping with our Tommaso," he said. "Heart's truth, my friend."

We all went to bed then, except Alfredo, who put on more hair oil and went off to visit somebody in one of the other vans.

That was the end of Wednesday, 15 July.

WHAT HAPPENED
ON 16 JULY 1942

We were woken up very early the next morning. At least Signor Corrado and I were. Nobody else seemed to hear the noise.

It was the policeman who sometimes helps out the Corrados. The one who sent off Pimply Arms and got the van to take Tommaso to the hospital. He banged on the door, really loudly, and shouted for Signor Corrado to come out. He said he needed to speak to him urgently. Signor Corrado went out but I couldn't hear what they were saying. Then the policeman must have gone away, because everything went quiet again.

Signor Corrado stayed outside for a long time. I could see him sitting on the step with his legs drawn up, because he hadn't closed the door completely. I suppose he was having a cigarette, because that was the first thing he did every morning. He came in at last.

"Are you awake, Jonas?" he whispered.

Of course I was! It was bright outside and I was just about ready to get up and leave so I could be back home before Mama and Papa got up for breakfast. I could go on my own. Anyway, Alfredo was fast asleep, with his mouth open to catch flies. The dogs were snoring. They were such clowns they'd forgotten dogs were supposed to bark at strangers making noise.

I got out from under the bed and piled my cushions up into a tower, but it fell over.

"Never mind that," Signor Corrado said. "Come over here to the table and sit down with me for a minute."

He looked pretty much the same as he'd looked the day before – all worried, with his beard showing through, like tar under his skin. Maybe he hadn't slept, for thinking about Tommaso.

But what he said was, "I'm afraid you can't go home, Jonas. There's been a police round-up, all over Paris. Of…"

He stopped there. I was staring at him because I thought he'd gone plain crazy. Of course I was going home. What else would I do?

Signor Corrado cleared his throat and got a whole lot of stuff up into his mouth. He went to the door to spit it out. Then he sat down again and took my hand in his.

"The police have rounded up Jews all over Paris," he said. "Our friend there, you know, who just called. Well, he knows about you, of course he does, because he's a policeman and they have special eyes out on stalks so they can see where to poke their noses. That's their job, poking their noses into other people's business."

This time he just spat into the corner.

"But that one, he's not bad. He came here to warn me. To warn *you*. You can't go home because your parents won't be there. They've been rounded up. The police have been on the go since four o'clock this morning."

I heard all these words but they made no sense. Why would anyone round up my parents? They hadn't done anything.

"But what about Nadia?" I said. "I'll have to go and get her. She'll be really scared there on her own."

I could hardly stand, I was shaking so much, but I found my sandals under the bed and started to put them on. Then Signor Corrado came over and put his hands on my shoulders and made me sit down.

"Look," he said. "It'll all prove to be a stupid

mistake, you'll see. Your parents are French, aren't they? They were born here, weren't they? When that lot find out they've made a mistake they'll let your parents go. And Nadia too."

They'd taken *Nadia*?

I nearly made it to the door then, but Signor Corrado caught me and held me, really tight. It hurt, so I kicked his shins but he wouldn't stop. He has extremely strong arm muscles and he just wouldn't let me go. Then I started to cry. He took one hand away and just rubbed my head, over and over.

"They'll let them go, Jonas," he said. "Don't worry. Nadia will be fine. They'll all be fine."

"But Papa was born in Germany!" I shouted at him. "That's why he didn't put his name down on their stupid list. It was so he wouldn't have to fight for the Germans!"

I didn't care who heard me. Anyway, everyone was awake now. La Giaconda came out of their little room and just stood there in her stripy pyjamas, staring at us. Alfredo was sitting up in his bunk and I could hear Madame Fifi saying soothing things to the dogs to calm them down.

"I'll make coffee," said La Giaconda. "Will you get the water, Jonas?"

"He won't," Signor Corrado said. "I'll do it. Lock the door after me."

He locked me inside the van for the rest of the day. Once I tried to get out through the window but he must have thought of that because it was nailed shut from the outside.

In the afternoon he sent Alfredo to rue des Lions, to see what he could find out. The problem was that Alfredo is not very good at doing things properly. Anyone could see that.

That's why I wondered for ages if Mama and Nadia were hiding under the bed or somewhere like that when Alfredo arrived at the house. I wondered if he knocked loudly enough, thinking Nadia might have felt the vibrations if he'd had a really good go at it.

When he came back Alfredo told us the main door to No. 7 was nailed shut and there was a big sign plastered across the lock. But he can't read French or German, only Italian.

He said nearly all the doors on the street were like that, and further up too, all along rue des Rosiers and rue Vieille du Temple. He said the signs looked a bit like circus posters.

"Only not cheery like ours, but with that ugly thick black print all crammed together. You know the kind."

Like the signs Nadia called the witchy signs.

KEEPING A PROMISE

⭐

When Madame Fifi came back from the meat market later on she said the policeman was right about the round-ups.

"I heard some really bad things," she said. She turned the corners of her mouth down, like a clown. "The poor people."

La Giaconda glared at her but she just shook her head. All that evening, every time she looked at me she shook her head again.

It was La Giaconda who told me I had to stay with the circus and keep myself safe.

"For Nadia's sake, Jonas, if not your own. Because when they let her go she's going to need you. You're going to have to be somewhere she can find you, and that's right here. There's no point in the whole of creation you getting rounded up too and sent off somewhere completely different. You just can't go back to your home."

She reached over and put my right hand across my chest. "I'm putting you on your honour, little Musketeer. Do you promise, hand on heart?"

So I stayed. I kept my promise. I worked away like before, helping with the circus. But it wasn't the same. Now I *really* wanted to go home in the evenings but my home was all locked up, with nobody in it.

When my fleas died I didn't bother burying them, like I used to. I just got more from Signor Corrado. I kept all the money I earned wrapped in a handkerchief under Alfredo's bed.

Tommaso came back home from the hospital after a few days. He was much deafer this time. He'd stare at you if you said something, and even though his eyes would get bigger you knew he couldn't understand almost anything you were saying. The thing was, even though he wasn't as deaf as Nadia, I was sure he wouldn't manage as well as she does.

One day I wrote a letter to Peppino, the footballer, like I'd promised. It was in French but it was supposed to be from Tommaso, so Signor Corrado turned what I'd written into Italian. He wrote it out on another piece of paper that had the Necker Hospital's name printed on it. He addressed the envelope to a football club in the city of Milan, in Italy. He wrote "Signor Giuseppe Meazza", not "Peppino". Then he posted it.

I told Tommaso and his parents about the sign language we used to talk to Nadia. I told them about her special school too, and how she really liked it because the teachers were clever and kind. Signor Corrado said he'd look into it for Tommaso before school started up again in September.

I said I'd help Tommaso out with all the signs I knew while I was waiting for my family to come back. But in the end I didn't get much of a chance because the policeman came round again. I didn't meet him that time either, because Tommaso and I were out kicking a ball around. But when he went away, Signor Corrado took me for a walk. He said he was going to have to find a new home for me.

"A house," he said. "It has to be a house, not a van. We have to find someone we can trust who will shelter Jonas Alber. Immediately."

Pimply Arms and his friends knew about me. One day a policeman had tried to arrest them for smashing the shutters on a shop, but they told the police captain he wasn't doing his duty. They said there was a boy with the circus who had no papers. Everyone knew what that meant, so why hadn't the Jew-lover done something about *that*, instead of arresting proper Frenchmen?

"The man is a savage," said Signor Corrado. "There are people like that in Italy too. But what it boils down to is that you're not safe here for a minute longer."

Well, my mother just never stopped doing her best, did she? She was so clever she'd given me that printed card the morning I left with Signor Corrado on the bike. The one with the Professor's name and address.

It was strange. I don't know why she did that. She'd never done anything like it before, all the Sunday mornings the Corrados had called to bring me to the fair at Nation. But that morning she did.

Here is something else that is strange: on the morning I came to the Prof's house Alfredo got up just as early as Signor Corrado and me, something he'd never done before. He took down his precious bottle of hair oil and rubbed some onto my hair. Only my hair is so straight it made it even flatter.

"See you around, little guy," he said.

It's getting even colder now. Our rooms in rue des Lions were cold too, but at least there you could snuggle up beside someone in your family. When you're cold on your own it's like being a tree in the park when everything is frozen stiff.

Even the spider has gone.

The Prof *does* allow me down for meals. And we have piano lessons every day. They're really the only good thing, apart from the encyclopedia. I know I'm playing better. Mama would be *really* pleased about that.

The Prof gave me a pair of gloves with the finger-tips cut off so I could practise without my hands falling off onto the floor. That's what happens to

Arctic explorers' hands if they forget and go out without their gloves.

The practice room is nearly as cold as my room upstairs because it faces north. None of the other houses look onto it, though, so that's a good thing. Nobody will peek in and say, *Who is that boy playing Beethoven with funny gloves on? We've never seen him before. We hope he has his papers.*

The Prof loves Beethoven the best so we play him the most. He showed me some music that a friend of his at the Conservatoire had written. It looked like ordinary music writing to me but the Prof said if you play it right it's supposed to sound like birds. His friend just loves birds. He goes into parks to listen to them and then tries to write down their songs so that people can play a blackbird song or a lark tune on the piano. It's quite a good idea but the music looked pretty hard to me.

Do birds know their songs are so difficult?

I asked the Prof what kind of sound an albatross makes but he didn't know. He thought it might be a screech, like a seagull, but I'm not so sure he's right. He said he'd ask his friend about it. I think an albatross would make a deep note like an organ, when all its stops are out. I mean a real organ like the one they have in the Notre-Dame Cathédral, not like the silly circus one.

One time Mama took all of us to hear a famous person play that organ. I don't remember what he played but it sounded like music that came all the way down from the skies just to bring you back up again with it. It filled up the whole huge space in the cathedral. It filled up your whole brain too. Even Nadia could hear bits of it, she said, though Mama said that was impossible.

Nothing is impossible for a willing heart. Didn't Mama remember that?

Jean-Paul thinks all people who play the organ are mad. He said the gargoyles that are stuck to the outside of old churches start out looking like normal statue people but all the organ music they have to listen to turns them into monsters after a few years. Papa said Jean-Paul never failed to astonish him.

Anyway, there was one gargoyle on the old church at the back of rue de la Harpe that I really liked. It was a beardy man holding up a goblin. The man looked like Monsieur Zacharides did when he was taking his bread out of the oven. Nadia thought so too, but we never told him in case we hurt his feelings.

I saw that gargoyle every day on my way to school. I used to see Monsieur Zacharides every day too.

23 OCTOBER 1942

ALBATROSSES

I've been reading a lot about albatrosses. They live all over the world wherever there are huge oceans for them to roam over. The biggest one is called the Wandering Albatross and the next biggest is the Southern Royal Albatross. When their wings are spread out they measure more than *three* metres. That makes them the biggest flying birds in the world.

If an albatross came to my window and if I let it in, it wouldn't be able to open its wings because the room here isn't big enough. Actually, I don't think it could fit through the window anyway, even with its wings folded. But I don't expect one will be coming along any time soon.

Tick the right reason:

No. 1 – because of the Germans

No. 2 – because there isn't enough fish in the markets

No. 3 – because Paris is not on the ocean

Albatrosses never feel the cold because they have special feathers. They love the bottom part of the Atlantic Ocean, near the Antarctic, but they fly across the Pacific Ocean too. They don't flap their wings. They glide.

They spend years out over the ocean, just flying around, watching ships and scooping up fish whenever they spot them. They like squid best of all. Sometimes sailors catch them by leaving out bits of meat on the deck, which is really mean because if an albatross is stuck on a ship in a storm he will get seasick, just like a human. It's true! Plus it's not a good idea anyway because it's really bad luck to catch an albatross.

Of course they have to come back to land to lay their eggs. They go to places like New Zealand and the cold part of Argentina and lay them near a cliff so that the first thing the chick will see when it hatches is the ocean.

The chicks take a long time to come out of the egg. It takes them about three days of banging on their shells to break it, not like a chicken who gets out really fast. That must be a bit scary for them, being stuck inside for three days, but I suppose it makes them very determined.

The parents feed the baby together but what they really want is to get it out to the ocean as soon as its wings are strong enough. That's the best place for an albatross. It's their real home. Still, it takes them quite a while to learn to fly. They're not good to begin with.

The encyclopedia says that albatrosses can fly millions of kilometres. So if they could breathe in space they could go to the moon and back. But they just like the ocean and all the fish.

Scientists think they live for a really long time too, like parrots and elephants. The scientists in New Zealand are going to catch some young albatrosses and put rings on their legs so they can work out how old they get. I hope they don't frighten them.

I'm sure Beethoven would have liked to write a sonata for an albatross if he'd known about them. He was a very lonely man and then he got deaf, which was terrible for him. Much worse than for Nadia because he used to be able to hear fine in the beginning, and also, of course, because he was a composer. But he did his best. The Prof says he could hear music in his brain instead of in his ears.

He just kept on going, like an albatross keeps on flying, across the frozen ocean.

I'm going to make an albatross for Nadia's theatre. I've asked the Prof to give me any leftover paper from his shopping. I'll soak that and make papier mâché out of it, the way Mama showed us. Nadia would really get a kick out of having a clever bird like that in one of her plays. We could paint scenes of a great frozen ocean, with icebergs at the back and the sides, and whales spouting foam from their blowholes.

Guess what? We'd have the cold for free.

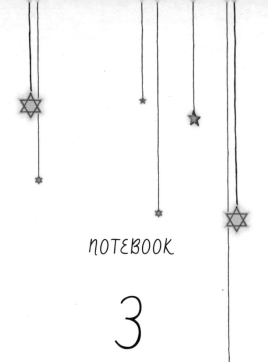

NOTEBOOK

3

I'll check the proper date later. I didn't feel like writing anything much until today.

No. 1 – I had a cold.

No. 2 – There was nothing to write about.

Today I saw a German motorcycle rider come down rue Cuvier. I was in my lookout position by the side of the window in my room, and there he was, really silent and deadly. The bike was black and silver and it gleamed in the sun.

One of the mirrors flashed a beam right through the gap in the curtain, onto the ceiling. It moved around until it was right above me. Like it knew I was there and it was an eye trying to search me out.

Then it passed on.

It wasn't a friendly motorbike like the ancient Lucifer that Monsieur Zacharides had. That made lots of really black smoke out of its middle and its rear end and it was always gasping and making very rude noises. You'd think it would explode any minute.

Sometimes Madame Perroneau got really mad with the noise it made and then Monsieur Zacharides would go back into the shop and come out with an éclair for her. Papa said Mama should complain about the Lucifer too, but she never did. She said Monsieur Zacharides was too nice for such a carry on. Anyway, he couldn't run his bike in the end because there was no more petrol.

This German motorbike wasn't fussy and noisy like the Lucifer. I thought it might skid and turn over because of the frost on the street but the driver was going too slowly for that. He seemed to be looking at the house numbers. I could hardly breathe until he'd gone way past No. 12.

About six or seven houses down the road, he stopped and got off and knocked at the door. I had to move to the other side of the window to see what he was doing. He had a big briefcase in his hand. He wore those trousers that stick out like jigsaw pieces, and tall black boots and a black leather coat. Then the door opened and he went in. I reckoned it was the same house the delivery man had gone to on the day of the burst water pipes.

The bike just stood there on its kickstand. You

knew nobody would mess with it, even if they wanted to kick it over or put sugar in its tank.

When I went down for dinner I told the Prof what I'd seen but it didn't seem to surprise him. He said that last week a really high-up German had moved into the house where the motorbike had stopped.

"My neighbour told me about it yesterday. It's someone who doesn't want to live in a hotel, like the rest of them do. It's meant to be a secret but everybody on the street must know about him by now."

"Is it Hitler?" I asked. Of course I didn't *really* think that but you never know till you ask.

The Prof just laughed. He never puts his hand up to his face these days. He is used to me.

"Pity it's not," he said. "We'd all help out with that one if it was. I'd say even old Grumpy next door would be willing to light a fuse or two."

I thought about the Prof and all the neighbours going down the road with a big round black bomb and leaving it on the German's doorstep. It really *was* a pity. Also, I have to confess that I wouldn't mind getting a look at Hitler for myself. Not many people get to do that, I bet.

But I was still bothered.

"Do you think they'll check all the houses on the

street?" I asked. "Do you think they already have? Maybe they burst the pipes just to get inside here and have a good look."

He wrinkled his nose a bit.

"I don't think so, Jonas," he said. "If they'd been serious about searching the house you can be sure they wouldn't have stopped with the kitchen. They don't have to pretend to be the fire brigade either. But I'll ask around to find out if anything has happened."

He chewed on his bread and honey for a while. "You know, in one way, that fellow makes everything safer for us because they'll already have checked us out. They'll want a nice peaceful street for Herr Prussian-Boots, whoever he is."

Oh, I *really* wanted to tell Nadia that name.

I told the Prof that Papa was born in Germany. "He isn't German, though, he's French," I said. "And he wouldn't speak any German to us. Mama thought that was a pity. She said then we'd be able to speak two languages and get ahead."

"Ah," he said.

Then he got up and went into his front room, where he hardly ever went. He came back with a photograph in a silver frame. It was of a woman with fair hair, like Mama, but this woman had hers done up on top of her head with a jewel kind of thing. She wore old-fashioned clothes but they were interesting. She looked pretty.

"My wife, Berthe," he said. "She was German. She was a singer. I have all her records but I can't listen to them any more. This photograph was taken in Berlin many years ago. That's where I met her."

"She looks nice," I said. I didn't really know what to say because she was dead now and that made him sad. Too sad to use the gramophone.

"She was," he said. "The war made her very unhappy. For all kinds of reasons. One was that she couldn't go back to see her family and that was lonely for her. She spoke very good French but she said she always thought and dreamed in German."

He took out a handkerchief and polished the glass of the photograph though it was pretty sparkly clean anyway, just as if Mama had been at it. Then he said something strange.

"I'm sorry you two never met, you and Berthe. She'd have liked you being in the house. She'd think it was just the right thing for me to do. She was always very kind to my pupils. She used to bake a cake on their birthdays."

Mama's birthday is 15 June. I wondered if Berthe had ever baked *her* a cake. But I didn't ask.

"The Nazis know that my wife was German,"

the Prof said. He always called the potato bugs *Nazis*. "They left us alone. Not that she was glad to see them in Paris, you understand. She would scold soldiers on the street if she saw them bullying people. She wasn't one to hold back, like I am." His voice had got a bit trembly.

"You didn't hold back with the fire brigade," I said.

"If only everything was that easy," he said, a bit sadly. "You eat up, and then we'll practise our Beethoven."

He brought the photograph along and put it on top of the piano in the practice room. Berthe looked happy there, I thought. She was able to hear music again, even if it wasn't exactly singing. Or very good either.

10 NOVEMBER 1942

OUT OF AFRICA

The Prof has found out some more about Herr Prussian-Boots down the road, though he didn't say how.

"When he was young he was a student in Paris and he worked in the Natural History Museum. That's why nowhere else would do him to live but rue Cuvier."

"Is that because it's close to the museum?" I asked.

Which it is. The museum with all the skeletons and fossils is straight across the park from this house. You can't see it from my room because the big conifer tree is in the way. You can't see the zoo either, but all the animals are gone, the Prof told me. He said they were in a safe place, just like I am.

Which really means *here* is not a safe place. But I didn't like to point that out to him.

"Probably," the Prof said. "But it might also be because our street is named after a famous scientist called Cuvier. He lived on this street, in one of the houses further down. Did you never notice the fountain at the top of the street? It's got lobsters and baboons and wolves and all sorts of other animals carved around the bowl. It's the Cuvier fountain."

I never had. Whenever we came to the park Papa only showed me the lion and that big old foot he was having for his lunch.

When the Prof went out I checked the encyclopedia and found out a few good things about Monsieur Georges Cuvier.

No. 1 – He discovered that Paris used to be under the sea. Millions of years ago. So that means there probably were albatrosses flying over here all the time. French albatrosses! He found this out by digging deep down under the streets and rivers and finding lots of shells and bones of sea animals.

No. 2 – He cut open cat mummies that Napoléon brought back from Egypt especially to show him. He said they were just ordinary pets that anyone would have. They weren't cat gods like the Egyptians thought they were. But imagine – Napoléon brought back cat mummies from the war! They never tell you those kinds of things in school, only about battles.

No. 3 – Cuvier found out that animals could become extinct. People used to think that God looked after everything all the time but it looks like he doesn't. Cuvier especially found this out about woolly mammoths. Everybody thought they were just stupid elephants, ones who wandered out of the jungle by mistake and went north where it was too cold for them. But they weren't. They were a different kind of creature entirely and now they're gone for ever, buried deep in the frost and snow.

When the Prof came home, he was full of news. Some lady at the Conservatoire had told him what she heard on the wireless from London last night. An army from Britain has invaded Africa to fight the Germans who are already there.

"That's a huge blow for the Nazis, Jonas," he said. "They're already fighting in Russia. That's two fronts."

I was working on the papier mâché albatross for Nadia's theatre. I'd been waiting for him, to ask if he had some paints or even just some blue ink so I could finish it off properly, with coloured-in feathers and eyes and a nice curvy beak. But he just sat down and told me more about the Africa thing.

I asked him what the wireless code messages had been this time but he didn't know.

"Maybe it was 'The camels have woken up at the oasis'," I said. "Or 'The ostriches' legs are growing longer'."

He thought they were good code messages but I knew Nadia would have thought of something better.

Our old neighbour Madame Perroneau had a Sunday hat with ostrich feathers on it, really soft and swishy-looking feathers. Nadia thought they were probably the best feathers in the world. She asked me to try to knock Madame Perroneau's hat off her head with my football so she could pick it up and feel the feathers, maybe even pull one off. I had to tell her it wasn't that easy. You could kill someone with a football and even if I hadn't killed Madame Perroneau, Mama would definitely have killed me if I'd knocked that hat off.

Now I wish I'd tried.

The Prof said I was the first person he'd told the Africa secret to and I'd probably be the last because pretty soon everyone would know and it wouldn't be a secret any more. The Nazis couldn't stop people talking, he said. And when the British ran them out of Africa, people would talk about that too.

"But of course you have to be careful who you

talk to, Jonas. Even an old man like me. There are some dodgy people around."

Well, *he* wasn't dodgy and *I* wasn't dodgy so right that moment I decided to ask him straight out if he'd found out anything new about my family, like he promised he would. Because it's been weeks since he's said anything about that.

And that's much more important than any old English army scaring the poor ostriches in Africa.

WHAT THE POLICEMAN KNEW

The Prof went over to the sink to get us some water. I didn't really want any but he put a cup in front of me anyway. We sat there, not drinking it.

"I didn't know who I could ask," he said, after ages, and one of his coughs. "I told you that I didn't want to go to the police and make any connection between you and me, especially when my plan is nearly worked out. So I went across the river to the fair the day before yesterday."

He'd been to the Corrados? And he hadn't told me anything? I was still staring at him when he started up again.

"You remember Signor Corrado's friend, the policeman?" he asked. He drank some more water.

I could see it going down his throat as if his throat were made of glass. He put down the cup but he didn't look at me this time. He was talking to the window.

"I'll tell you what the policeman told Signor Corrado, Jonas. Signor Corrado wasn't sure if I should tell you, but there it is. Now you've asked me, I will."

I didn't take my eyes off him.

"Signor Corrado has been pestering that policeman for weeks to find out what has happened to your family," he said. "Just a short while ago he came back and told Signor Corrado what he'd found out. Something only a policeman could do, it seems."

More water going *glug, glug, glug* down.

"After the round-up, your parents were sent down the country somewhere. Then they were brought back to Paris again, with all the other people. And now they've been sent off to work. He doesn't know where. There are different places, apparently."

He coughed then, even after all that water. He was coughing so much he didn't hear what I'd asked and I had to shout it again.

"Nadia can't work! Who'll look after her? She's only little and she's deaf!"

It was odd but he looked a bit happier then. He stopped looking out of the window and looked at me.

"Well, that's the thing," he said. "The policeman's wife has a sister who works with deaf children. The night before the round-up he told her about a little Jewish girl he knew about who was deaf. That was your Nadia, of course. He'd seen her on her birthday at the fair. You told me all about that day, remember?"

I just kept staring at him so he wouldn't be able to look away again.

"He told this woman, his wife's sister, that Nadia was a lovely little thing, bright as a button, and it was a terrible pity about what was going to happen to all the Jewish families the next day, and he was just telling her about this one girl."

Cough.

"He said his sister-in-law went out very early that morning, and left while it was still dark. That's all he knows because she won't talk to him any more even though she lives in the same house. He told Signor Corrado he doesn't know what happened exactly but he *does* know that Nadia's name is not on any list. He doesn't think she was in the vélodrome at all."

"The vélodrome? What do you mean? What list?"

The Prof looked like he might be sick.

"The Vél d'Hiv, that big cycling stadium down near the Eiffel Tower. That's where the police took everybody they rounded up on 16 July. They kept them there for five days. Your parents were there, the policeman knows that, because there's a list that has their names on it. But, like I said, there was no sign that Nadia was ever there."

He picked up the albatross. It was still wet, so the big wings drooped right down. It didn't matter.

"So that's good news, because it looks as if she's probably hidden and safe, just like you, Jonas. In fact, she's probably making puppets right now at a kitchen table somewhere. Like you."

"But she's deaf!" Did he not understand *anything* important? "She needs Mama or Papa or me! They always said I had to look out for her if they weren't around. Hardly anybody in the world knows how to do sign language."

"Of course they said that," the Prof said. "And they were right. But it just didn't work out that way. I'm sorry. This woman works with deaf children so she would understand about your sister. That's all I know. I'm glad you asked. I was going to tell you as soon as I knew about the other business."

He put the albatross down again, carefully.

"I'm sorry, Jonas. But you must keep your hopes

up. Signor Corrado said I was to tell you that. Which reminds me."

He took out a piece of crumpled paper from his jacket pocket.

"He said to give you this. He said Tommaso got a signed letter from this person. And they all send their love."

I straightened out the paper. There were just two words on it, in big black printy handwriting.

"GIUSEPPE MEAZZA."

I put my head right down on the table. I knew I was squashing the albatross good and proper but I didn't care. I didn't care about the Prof, or Signor Corrado or Tommaso and his footballer's letter, or anybody else. I only wanted my family to be together.

But we had all disappeared.

THE SALMON OF KNOWLEDGE

Paris is as big as an ocean. If you were an ant in the forest at Vincennes you couldn't even imagine Paris. You'd think your bit of sandy path was the whole world and all you had to do was fight off other ants who tried to get into it. Or if you were one of Madame Fifi's dogs, you'd think the world began at the circus in Nation and ended at the meat market in Les Halles. You wouldn't even know there were animals like cows and pigs that had made the meat.

My poor fleas too. I reckon they thought a human arm was like heaven because it was huge and full of nice hot blood. I don't know what they thought of pulling carriages, though. Probably that was hell for fleas, now that I think of it. I feel sorry about that.

When we lived in rue de la Harpe I knew the way to my school and Nadia's school and the park and the Luxembourg Gardens, and where our doctor lived, and down to the river, and across the bridge to the cathédral, and back to the métro station at Cluny.

But I'd only been to the fairground, oh, maybe twice. I'd never even heard of rue des Lions. Or rue des Rosiers, where the Jewish families who were very religious lived, where some of the boys my age had long curls at the side of their head and wore hats and funny black suits.

I know those places now. The map in my head has got bigger.

I guess when the small eels begin to leave the Sargasso Sea they don't really know their way to the rivers where they'll grow up. They just set out one day and the more they swim the bigger the map in their head gets and pretty soon they find out where they have to go.

Salmon do it too, except the other way round. They're fully grown up when they swim all the way across the Atlantic Ocean. What they want is to get home to the rivers they were born in. When they find the right river they swim right to the top of it and breed and then they die, even though some of them have got really big in the ocean, maybe as long as a man's leg. They find their way because they grow a map like the eels do.

The Prof's mythology book says that long ago in Ireland, the basking shark country way out in the Atlantic Ocean, there was once a very famous salmon. It was so big and old it knew everything in the world, even algebra and constellations. All the people knew that the person who ate the salmon would swallow all its knowledge and know everything too. One day a king caught it and gave it to his servant to cook. But when the servant was turning the salmon over he burned his hand on the skin and sucked the burn, swallowing a piece of fish skin. Guess what, it was bad luck for that king because the servant knew everything then.

Mama used to say fish was good for our brains so maybe that story is a bit true. I like fish but Nadia hates it. It doesn't matter because she knows lots of things anyway.

The problem is that ever since I came here my world has got small again. Now it's just got four sets of stairs, a table room, a piano room, a bedroom and a trunk. And the window. I'm nearly as bad as the circus dogs, except that I've got my memory. I'm sure I could still get to all the places I used to know. But what about the places I don't know? There won't be time to grow a new map. You have to be travelling and doing things to grow a map.

And there isn't much time because the Prof says my new papers are nearly ready.

So I'll only have one chance to find out exactly what happened to Nadia. I need to know for sure.

WHO IS GRÉGOIRE VOLET?

The identity papers are the Prof's famous Plan. It's taken him a long while to work it out. I've been here in this house since the 23 August and now it's well into November.

The Prof has a friend who lives somewhere in Normandy. The friend had a boy who was a bit younger than me but he died of some disease last spring because there was no proper medicine in the hospital he went to. That was awful for everyone, but after the boy's funeral his family kept his identity card. They didn't use it to get food but they couldn't bear to throw it away either, the Prof said. He knew all about it and that was how he started to make his plan.

Last month the Prof's friend came to Paris to play some music in a concert. The two of them met at the concert and they started talking about Guess Who:

No. 1 – Robin Hood.

No. 2 – The Boy Who Knows Nothing Any More.

No. 3 – (Sorry, I can't think of any No. 3 right now.)

The Prof didn't ask his friend straight out for the identity card. He'd never do that, he said. It would be *insensitive*. But he told him lots of things, about me being on my own and how great it would be for me to be in a proper family.

Well, I could see some problems there.

"What about all the people in Normandy?" I asked when he first told me about his plan. "They'll know I'm not the boy who died! I wouldn't even look like his ghost!"

But the Prof said his friend was moving with his family to a different town, to share a house with his sister and her family. Rouen was the new town.

"That's the beauty of it, Jonas. The people in Rouen won't know the boy is dead. And the Nazis there won't know any better. It's a big port. They have other things to worry about."

I asked him what the dead boy's name was.

"Grégoire Volet," he said.

I said that a few times in my head. It was the same length as my name. But nothing like it.

The Prof had been Grégoire's godfather but he'd met him only once, when he was just a baby. The Prof looked really sad. It's rotten when anybody dies, even if they were only a baby when you met them, long before they started to do anything much.

He took my left hand and pressed it out on the kitchen table, like when we did stretch exercises for our hands. His fingers were as light as twigs.

"Jonas, I will miss you," he said. "A lot. You can't imagine. I told you how Berthe would be so pleased I took you in. I'm very glad myself. I like to think we are good friends. I mean that. But because you're my friend I want you to be safe, and I promise you that you'll be much safer with papers, and out of Paris."

He said if I went to Normandy I'd be able to go outside and play and have a normal life like any other boy in France. I could go to school again.

"You'll learn much more than you ever will just reading my old encyclopedias at the kitchen table."

"But I *like* doing that!" I said. "And I really like playing the piano with you."

"That's the best bit," he said. He was beaming. "My friend has plans to start a children's orchestra in Rouen, even now, in these dark days. You could learn the flute with him. For your mother's sake. Didn't you tell me that was what she wanted?"

I didn't answer that. Yes, Mama had said I could choose my instrument. But I was only going to choose it when she was there.

I wasn't a bit sure about the plan anyway.

"Why not have Grégoire Volet's card sent to Paris and then I can stay here and pretend to be him, here? After all, you're his godfather, right? We could just go on as we are doing now only I could go out to the park."

The Prof shook his head, slow first, then faster.

"No, no, Jonas," he said. "It's not safe for you. Please, please, take my word for it. I've thought a lot about all of this. I can't send you to school anywhere near here. It would be too tricky and you could be spotted by anybody at any time. What about that awful man at the circus? And suppose something happened to me. What would you do then?"

"But what about this Grégoire's brothers and sisters? They'll know I'm not him. They'll tell people about me. And what could happen to *you*?"

He looked at me as if I'd slapped him. I'd forgotten he was so old. He could die of course. He didn't say anything for ages. Then he did but his voice sounded a bit peculiar.

"My apologies, Jonas. I forgot to tell you that Grégoire had just one little brother and he's far too young to remember anything, or even to talk. He's not even two. Grégoire was eight."

"But I'm ten!"

We both knew that didn't matter. I'm small for my age and there's no getting away from that.

I knew he wouldn't have an answer for my final question. *Because he just didn't know.*

"What about Nadia? La Giaconda said I had to stay put for her. If she's safe like you say, she'll be waiting for me to come and get her."

I was right. He didn't have an answer. Not a proper one. He just said that if Nadia went to see the Corrados and then turned up here he'd be able to tell her I was safe and sound. "And, if I'm spared, when the war is over I'll bring her down to Rouen myself."

He said his friend would be coming to the house in a couple of days, bringing Grégoire's identity card, and he'd take me away with him then.

"You're going to escape, Jonas," he said. "That's what matters now. You're not going to be anybody's prisoner any more."

And that was the end of it. Maybe it is even a good plan. Anyway, it is all arranged.

LAST CHANCE

The Prof had to leave in a rush this morning. It's a long way to the Conservatoire and he said the métro hadn't been very obliging the last time he used it.

Papa hated the métro. He liked to walk or cycle whenever he could. Nadia hated it too because sometimes the noise used to get inside her head. But Mama and I both loved it. I loved the electric smell down there, and the way the trains burst into the station and are so eager to get going again, like husky dogs pulling a sledge, or something. Mama liked the way you never quite know where you'll come out if you stop at a station you don't know. She said the métro was a proper Underworld. But

I can't remember when we were last down there.

When the Prof was gone I went upstairs and took my money out of the trunk. I had more than 200 francs, all in coins. I didn't know what a métro ticket cost any more but that was probably enough for quite a few journeys. I just had to hope the policeman didn't live very far out of town.

I had one of Robert's pullovers on, with two vests underneath it. And my suit, which wasn't scratchy any more because it had got used to me. I didn't have a coat. I looked inside the Prof's wardrobe but there was nothing useful there except a grey woollen scarf and one of his hats. I thought the hat might hide my eyes but it was so big it looked like a bucket over my face. The scarf was better. I wound it over my mouth, my nose and my ears and looked at myself in the mirror. Well, it was winter. People wore scarves to keep warm, didn't they?

I couldn't do anything much about my eyes or my hair but there's nothing special about them. Except my hair had got long. La Giaconda was the last person to give me a haircut, the night before I came here. I took the scissors from the Prof's dressing table and cut right across the fringe. It looked straight enough.

The best thing was to look ordinary. You could

disguise yourself completely if you painted a clown face, say, but then everybody would look at you. Besides, certain people *had* to recognize me or they wouldn't tell me what I needed to know.

I brushed my shoes with the Prof's shoe polish set. He was fussy about his shoes so he had a selection of different tins. I hoped the shoes would be all right to walk in. It was more than three months since I'd walked anywhere that wasn't inside a house. But Mama always said it was a mercy that my feet grow slowly. Jean-Paul's shoes were always about three sizes bigger than mine.

I left a note for the Prof on the kitchen table. I wouldn't be able to get inside the house again until he got back. I had no key. I didn't want him going crazy with worry about me so I wrote just a short thing.

Dear Professor,

I've gone out to see if I can find out more about Nadia and get a message to her. Don't worry, I'll be very careful. I've taken one of your music cases to look like a proper student and I have your map of Paris inside it in case I need to go somewhere I don't know.

I'll be back before it gets dark. If you're not in when I get back I'll walk around the park – inside if it's open, outside if it's locked.

See you later (and don't worry again).

Jonas

PS There are some things in the trunk you should look at if I get delayed for a long time.

I opened the front door but before I even got a chance to look at anything I had to close it again. It wasn't the cold air. And there wasn't anything wrong with my plan. During the night I'd thought of pretty well everything. If someone were to stop me, I'd explain that I just didn't have my papers right then. I was visiting my godfather and somehow he forgot to give them to me because he's pretty old. But I would have them tomorrow.

The trouble was, the minute I opened the door I knew my story was useless because I hadn't found out enough facts.

Oh, your name is Grégoire Volet, is it? Spell that for me, I'm a Nazi. What school do you go to in Normandy? What station did you arrive at in Paris? Do your parents have a telephone? Why not, if they're music teachers? What are their names?

It was no good. There was nothing I could do about any of that now. What I could do was go out and give it a try. Or I could stay in, like every other day, and nothing would happen. The truth was today was my last chance. I took six deep breaths and opened the door again.

Grégoire Volet would have to be the most stupid boy in France. Or maybe the most scared. After all, one of the Kamynski girls hadn't been able to speak for a week after a soldier stuck his gun in her back to frighten her. It wasn't hard to play scared.

But why should Grégoire be afraid? He had nothing to worry about. (Except that he's dead.)

I'd already made up my mind which way to turn, because it wouldn't look good if I didn't know where I was going when I came out of the house. But in case there was something going on outside I tipped all the music out on the step, just to get a few seconds to look around.

I hadn't asked the Prof which side his mean neighbour lived on. But that was all right. If he was looking out, at last he'd be able to see who'd been making all that awful noise on the piano this past while. And what would he say?

That's a very nervous boy. Look at him fumbling with those pages. What's the matter with him?

I'd checked the map last night. It was much shorter to go left, down the street to the river, and cross at the bridge. The long way was to go right, up the street, turn into the park and go all the way through it until you came to the same bridge. That way was nicer and there would probably be no soldiers. Plus I'd see my lion. But suppose I ran into someone from my old school? It would be no help having the scarf wrapped around my face like a bandit. We used to do that all the time when we played cowboys and we always knew who everyone was.

I turned left.

My legs were pretty wobbly, a bit like they'd been after I had the measles. But at least my shoes didn't pinch too much. There was ice on the pavement slabs but the shoes had good thick heels, which was just as well. A woman coming up the road slipped and went down. When she got up again her shoe heel was broken.

There were two potato bugs standing outside Prussian Boots's house. But there was no flag. The stupid man probably thought nobody would know about him if there was no flag. I moved the music case to my left hand so the soldiers could see it. I just stared straight ahead when I passed them, like any proper French person would. They didn't care. They were laughing at the woman who had to limp by in her broken shoe.

Then I was at the bottom of the street and the bridge was ahead. There was no checkpoint. I should be safe until I got to the fairground.

THE WOMAN
IN THE FUR COAT

On the bridge it was much colder because the wind was whipping hard along the river, turning over little grey waves below. I had to keep the music case down by my side so that everybody could see it, but I kept my other hand stuffed into my jacket pocket to keep it warm. I kept going by thinking of the hot air that was waiting for me in the métro station.

I was halfway across, when a woman coming towards me stopped right in the middle of the path and looked at me. She was big, and she was staring *really* hard at me. I moved to pass her but she grabbed my shoulder to stop me. She had pointy black leather gloves, like claws.

"Why are you not in school, dear?" she said. "Do you live near here?"

She was a German! She wasn't one of the ones in uniform, she was just an ordinary woman. But you could tell she was German by the way she spoke French – very loud, and moving her mouth too much.

A man stopped to watch, even though it was so cold on the bridge. The German woman looked rich. She had a long fur coat on and lots of red lipstick. Why had she stopped me? I hadn't done anything. I was just walking. It wasn't this woman's business that I wasn't in school. She wasn't a school inspector, was she?

Maybe she was.

I lifted up the music case to show her. "I have to do my piano exam today," I said. "At the Conservatoire."

I didn't know if I should call her "Madame" or if there was another word you should use for German women. The Prof would know that kind of thing. But if I was being rude she didn't seem to notice.

"Surely you're not going to walk all that way, child?" she said. "That thin tweed isn't fit for this weather. Look at your knees. They're purple! What was your mother thinking to let you out like that?"

"She's in hospital," I said. "Anyway, I have my father's scarf. I'm not cold."

The man who'd stopped to watch laughed. "Fighting words, son!" he called out to me. "Now ask the lady about the lovely weather her mates have in Russia." Then he ran off, laughing.

The woman looked after him. There were two red spots on her cheeks. If she'd had a whistle I bet she'd have blown it to get soldiers to come and chase after him. But she had only me.

She wrapped her fur coat even tighter around herself with one hand. The other one still gripped my shoulder. Until she let it go and pulled at my scarf instead.

"I want to see your face," she said. "Maybe I know you if you live near here."

I stared back at her. Maybe there was a photograph of me somewhere, like the gangster photographs policemen had in American films.

Have you seen this Jewish boy?

The woman took the ends of my scarf and wrapped them around my head, covering my ears. I could smell the leather of her gloves. The fur cuffs brushed my face, the way Grimaldi's tail did when you stroked him. She fastened the scarf inside my collar at the back, pushing it right down.

"Don't snivel, boy," she said. "You're a musician.

It's written all over your face, even though you're so young. And music is a privilege."

She started fumbling inside her fur coat. She wasn't holding me any longer but I didn't dare move. Even though she was quite old I'd say she'd have caught me again, I was so petrified.

"But it's shocking that you're not better cared for. Here, I'm going to give you something."

She took out a purse and from it a banknote. She pressed it into my hands.

"Here, boy. Take the métro. The train will take you straight all the way." She pointed. "Over there. If you don't do that you'll get so cold you simply won't be able to perform at all. Believe me, I know these things. Good luck with your exam."

She was gone before I could say anything, even thank you.

I looked at the banknote. It was so long since I'd seen one. Fifty francs. There were some words right under the person's picture. They were printed to look like old-fashioned handwriting and they were spelled in a funny way. But guess what they said:

"Nothing is impossible for a willing heart."

Mama's words. It was a message. Not from the wireless but from a real live German.

Gone, gone, gone, gone, gone

But there was no yellow van at the Foire du Trône.

There was just a shape cut into the ground where it had stood and where the grass was still flattened. There were no Corrados.

I went down the street, looking at all the other vans. I recognized the ones that belonged to the strongman, the fortune teller, the tumblers. But none of the vans was the nice yellow of a fried egg on a pan and they all had their doors closed. Even if I wasn't supposed to be in hiding I'd never have dared knock on one. It was much too early. There were only a few people walking on the street and just a couple of men coming along the path on bicycles. Where was Papa's bicycle now?

I felt sick.

The kiosk at the top of Cours de Vincennes was open. I could see Violette inside, with her big yellow hair. She was talking to an old man, giving him cigarettes. When he moved off I pushed the scarf down from my face and went over to the kiosk.

"Where's Alfredo gone?" I asked her. "The Corrados' van isn't there."

She looked at me as if I had something wrong with my head.

"Don't you know? They've gone off to Neuilly. This place wasn't good enough any more, they said. Truth was, everybody was sick of their stupid tricks. That greasy tramp, the one whose name you mentioned, can go and jump in the river for all I care. So don't come talking to me about those people."

It was a really bad word she called Alfredo. It wasn't *tramp*.

"How do you get to Neuilly?" I asked. "Is it in Paris?"

But suddenly Violette wasn't looking at *me*. Her eyes were fixed on something behind me and she looked a bit frightened. I turned round.

Pimply Arms.

Not that you could see his arms now, because

he was dressed in a long black coat. It was open at the front and there was a long stick hanging from his belt, like the ones policemen wear. I didn't need to see his arms. I knew his face straightaway, even though if you'd asked me a minute before what he looked like I couldn't have said. It was just the worst face.

He came right up and put his hands round my neck until the fingers met at the back. He didn't even have to squeeze to do that, his hands were so big. Then he took them away and held tight to my arm.

"Welcome back, little flea-boy – *Jonas Alber*." he said. He tipped his cap to Violette. "Thanks for that, Violette. You could have told him to scram, and he might have made it."

Violette began pulling down the wooden shutter of the kiosk. She was nearly crying. "I did nothing to help you, you creep! Nothing!"

Pimply Arms laughed. "Better keep the place open for the troops, Violette! They won't like to see you all closed up so early."

She banged the ~~shutter~~ closed. "Devil!" she shouted. Already she sounded far away.

"It was good of you to come out of your mouse hole," Pimply Arms said to me. "Important people were looking for you. Now we're going to take a little walk. And on the way you're going to tell me where you've been all this time. And who was stupid enough to take in vermin like you."

He started pulling me along with him towards the big roundabout at Nation. My feet must have been doing something to keep up with him but I couldn't feel them moving. My brain wasn't working at all. It was frozen.

"You don't know my real name," I managed to say. "Jonas Alber is just a stage name."

He laughed again but not as much as before. "Don't try to be smart. It won't help you."

"Do you think Madame Fifi's parents called her that when she was a baby?" I asked. "That's a stage name."

He pinched my arm. "Funny that the rest of your family was called Alber. I wonder where they've all got to now, don't you?"

He noticed the music case then because it kept hitting against his leg. He stopped.

"What have you got there? Give it here."

Music cases have a special bar. It's a really simple thing but Pimply Arms had no idea how to work it, especially because he was using only one hand. He was keeping the other one fastened like a hook to my arm.

"Open it, you," he snarled. "And don't try anything or I'll hand you over to our masters in pieces.

Where'd you get a good leather bag like that anyway? You stole it. Look!"

I'd taken the case from the piano room but I hadn't noticed the name printed in funny gold letters on the flap. Berthe Weiss. It had to be the Prof's wife's name. Just as well the German woman on the bridge hadn't spotted *that*. She was so fond of music she might have known Berthe Weiss, the famous singer.

I opened the bar. Then, just like before, I flipped the case over and emptied the music all over the path. Pimply Arms thumped the side of my head, really hard.

"Pick those papers up, you filthy brat. On your knees."

He let my arm go but that was only so he could knock me over, which he did. Then he kicked me until I was kneeling and he pressed his big booted foot hard on my back to keep me there. The ground wasn't just freezing, it was covered with frozen lumps. Stones, I suppose, but they felt like pieces of ice cutting into me.

I sneaked a look around. There was still nobody much out walking. I guess the people who didn't have to work were staying in bed to keep warm. At least there weren't any soldiers anywhere near. There was very little traffic at the roundabout.

We'd got quite close to the métro station entrance but it was still a street across from where we were. I didn't think Pimply Arms planned to take the métro, because then he'd have to pay for me. He didn't know about the money I had in my pocket. Not yet, anyway.

I picked up all the music sheets and put them sitting on top of the case, as if it was a tray. Then I stood up. My knees were skinned and cut. I could feel the blood trickling down into my socks, but the funny thing was how warm it felt. My blood was the warmest thing I had.

I held the case out to Pimply Arms. That way he'd need two hands to take it, even if it was only for a second. But he didn't move to hold it. All the time I'd been picking up the music he'd kept one hand on his stick. Now he took it from his belt.

"Are you mocking me, you little piece of dirt?" he said.

"Look!" I shouted. "The parachute! Coming down over there!"

He stared at me and then, even though you could see he knew he shouldn't, he turned all the way round, to look where I was pointing.

I dropped the case hard on his feet and ran.

UNDERWORLD

I suppose the salmon and the eels don't worry too much about all the dangers in the Atlantic Ocean. Or all the fishermen waiting for them on the rivers. If they did worry they'd be too scared to set out at all and the whole Atlantic Ocean would get clogged up until they all died, and then there'd be none left. No, they just stick to what they know and off they go, with their fishy maps.

It's not that easy for humans, though.

No. 1 – We don't know exactly where we're going most of the time.

No. 2 – We keep thinking about the bad things that can happen.

No. 3 – It's easier to see a human running than

something that's covered up by the whole ocean.

But I was much faster at running than Pimply Arms was. He was a bit fat to start with, and you can bet his big coat was no help. He kept shouting for people to stop me but I don't think they liked the sound of him because nobody lifted a hand to grab me. When I'd reached the bottom of the métro stairs there was still no sign of him arriving at the top. I didn't worry about buying a ticket this time. I just wriggled under the bar and ran down one of the corridors, towards the platforms.

Nobody saw me dodging under, or if they did they didn't care.

There's a really small boy. He's dead scared of something. Let's leave him alone.

There was a train waiting, with all its doors open. The really strange thing was that it was exactly like a fairground Ghost Train because the very second I jumped into the carriage, the doors slid over and the train moved off. It was weird, but you couldn't have asked for better help from a train.

I crouched down below the window and pretended to be fixing my shoe, so that Pimply Arms or the station men couldn't see me if they made it as far as the platform. Then we were in the tunnel and I could stand up again. I didn't care where the train was going. All I had to decide was where to get off. But definitely not the first station because that would still be too close to Nation.

I stayed standing, near the doors, but there was a woman sitting opposite who kept staring, first at my knees and then at all the rest of me because I was still breathing so fast. The blood had got all crusty now and I suppose that made my knees look even worse.

"I fell down the steps," I said to the woman. "I'm late for my music exam."

Then I remembered I didn't have the music case any more. But the woman didn't seem to notice that.

"Oh dear," she said. "Here, use this." She gave me a handkerchief. "Spit on it and rub," she said. "Sit down. It'll be easier."

So I sat beside her and cleaned up my knees as best I could. They were getting stiff now. I wasn't sure I could run if I had to, even though my breathing was nearly normal again.

"I'm sorry about the handkerchief," I said.

She got up. "You can keep it, but take better care of yourself next time. Remember, being late is much better than being dead."

I was sorry to see her go because it had looked like we were together, even if it was only for a short time.

I didn't recognize any of the station names until

we came to the stop for the cemetery. My Granny Berlioz is buried there. One time, when we still lived in rue de la Harpe, Mama brought Nadia and me there. Not Jean-Paul, though he really wanted to come. It was for Granny's birthday, even though she was dead. Mama brought sandwiches and some peaches in a bag and we sat on one of the seats to have our picnic. Then Nadia spent ages following a black cat around and I had a good look at the really old gravestones. The best one had a statue of a man who was killed in a duel. He was lying flat with his pistol beside him, and his hat that had fallen off when he was shot. The hat and the pistol were all part of the statue. I told Jean-Paul about it when we got back but he said I was making it up.

A lot of people got on the train at that stop. Two German soldiers all in black pushed their way on, ahead of everyone. They squeezed themselves beside an old woman but she mustn't have liked that one little bit because she got up and came down to stand near me. I didn't want the soldiers to notice me but I got up and gave the woman my seat because it would have looked worse if I hadn't. Anyway, the soldiers didn't even notice.

I had my scarf tight around my face again. I didn't even have to pretend I was cold because I was shivering so much. Everyone else kept their heads down or looked at the dark windows.

I got off at the first station that had another line going through it. There was a bit of a wait for the next train on that line, which was not good. I didn't think Pimply Arms could know where I was now but he might have got a message to all the métro people. *Stop the boy in the brown suit and the grey scarf.* And I had no ticket either, if anyone came along checking for them.

I stood behind the tallest people I could find. They were two nuns wearing long robes and huge stiff white hats with two peaks. From where I was the hats looked like albatross wings. I bet people thought I was an orphan, standing there behind the nuns, but that would be a good thing. I just hoped they would continue travelling in the same direction as me and not go somewhere peculiar.

The platform was the warmest place I'd been since I left the Prof's kitchen. The more people that crowded onto it, the warmer it got. Everyone got pressed together. I hadn't seen anybody except the Prof for so long that it was a bit strange to see so many other people, and all at once too. I didn't want anyone to touch me, even by accident. I pulled in my shoulders and kept my hands in my pockets.

I kept staring hard at the nuns' backs. One of them had a tear in her robe that was sewn up with yellow thread, exactly the colour of the stars Jews had to wear. There were ten and a half tiny stitches. *10a*. Our address in rue des Lions. Somebody shoved me to the side but I got back again, standing behind the nuns. I really didn't want to catch anybody's eye because even if they're not looking for you people can be bossy. But if they thought I was with the nuns, and if the nuns didn't know I was standing behind them, I'd be all right.

I just wished there were some other children around to take people's minds off me. There was only one other boy that I could see, standing near the edge of the platform, but he was older, maybe fourteen, and he had long pants and a school bag.

The big iron barrier clanged across the passageway, to stop any more people running onto the platform. That gave me a fright because I'd forgotten how loud a noise it makes, like something in a dungeon. Then I could hear wheels humming, getting louder, and smell the wind and the sparks, and the train rushed out of the tunnel, all in a mad hurry to get to Châtelet. That was the station I'd picked, to come up out of the métro. It was near the river and I knew how to find my way back to the Prof's house from there.

Châtelet was the station that always hurt Nadia's ears the most because it was so huge and had so many different passages. There was always more noise and more wind there than anywhere else. Even Mama could get lost down there. She said you always had to keep your wits about you at Châtelet, and mind your purse too.

I stuck with those nuns, even though they got seats on the train and I had to stand. I stood beside them, all the way. They didn't look at me and they didn't speak to each other. I suppose they were praying hard, with their arms folded inside their long robes. Just like the old priest we used to see, walking around in the church behind rue de la Harpe. Where Mama had made me promise to bring Nadia, if anything ever happened to her and Papa.

Oh, Mama, I tried my best. I really tried, but it didn't work.

HOME

It was starting to snow by the time I reached rue Cuvier. That made the whole sky dark, even though I knew it couldn't really be very late. It didn't feel as cold as it had been earlier but I had to keep brushing the flakes off my hair and my shoulders or else I would have turned into a snowman. I wrapped the scarf around my head but it didn't take long before it got as wet as a dishcloth.

There was no guard outside Prussian-Boots's house this time.

I gave a little tap on the door of No. 12. Nothing happened. I felt terrible. The park would be a really scary place to have to wait in now. *Why is that boy standing under the trees in the snow? Has he no home*

249

to go to? Besides, the park people would probably lock up the gates so they could get back to their own homes before the snow got worse. I'd have to keep walking around and around outside, just like I'd said in my note. And I was starving.

I peeked through the letterbox. Nothing, just darkness. I'd forgotten the Prof had nailed a black cloth across it after the day with the firemen. I tried to poke the cloth out of the way but it wasn't easy.

I was so busy doing that I nearly fell on my face when the door opened wide. The Prof grabbed me by the arm and pulled me inside. He closed the door and leaned back against it, breathing very hard. His face was as white as the ceiling.

"It's all right," I said. "I'm really, really sorry, but I had to do it. I couldn't tell you beforehand because you wouldn't have let me go. I'm all right, I promise. It didn't work out but I had to try."

He still said nothing, just put one hand on my cheek, as if he was petting me.

"You're frozen," he said. "My God in heaven, but I prayed for you, Jonas Alber. It's a long time since I prayed for anybody in that way."

Then he just grabbed me in a big clutch with both hands and held me to him. He said nothing more. His clothes smelled of the kitchen, steamy and damp.

"Come down," he said. "We have a visitor."

The kitchen was bright and warm. I'd never realized a room could be so warm, not since we lost our home. The little flame on the gas felt like a blazing campfire. There was a pot of something on top, boiling away, and a big loaf cut into slices on the table.

There was a woman sitting in the seat I usually sat in. Her coat was draped over the table, covering my encyclopedias. She reminded me of someone, but I couldn't think who it was. I'd never seen her before. I'd never seen *anybody* in the Prof's house all the time I'd been here.

I didn't want anyone to be there on my last night with the Prof.

"This is Jonas, Nadia's brother," the Prof said to the woman. "Jonas, say hello to Madame Picard, who has very kindly come here to give us some information."

Nadia's brother? I was still trying to figure out why he had said that when he reminded me to shake hands.

"My goodness, but your hands are frozen, young man," the woman said. She shook her head and looked cross. "Going out like that was very unwise. This poor man was driven wild with worry. And though I haven't been in the house for long I was getting that way too. You see, I have somebody else to think about."

Then she did something very peculiar. She lifted her hands up and signed to me. When she'd finished I kept staring, not because I'd forgotten how to read the signs but because of what she'd said. The Prof hadn't noticed.

"Here," he said. "Wrap this rug around you and I'll go upstairs and get you some fresh clothes. Then we'll have to get everything you're wearing dry for tomorrow."

He stopped at the door. "Madame Picard, would you mind serving Jonas some of the soup?"

Ten minutes ago I had been dreaming of eating something hot. Now all I could think about were the words she'd signed.

I know what happened to Nadia.

Who did this woman think she was – La Giaconda? I stared hard at her. She was ordinary. She couldn't possibly know anything about Nadia. I'd spent all day dodging Pimply Arms and Germans, trying to pretend I was an orphan, trying not to freeze to death, and this woman had just called here and thought she knew something about my sister? She mustn't know how to sign properly. She'd made a mistake.

She put a bowl of soup in front of me.

"I think you may have heard of me, Jonas," she said. "My brother-in-law is a policeman. Not a bad one, but not the best either. Could do better. You know who I mean?"

I nodded.

"Take your soup. I won't say another word till you've taken at least three spoonfuls."

She was so bossy. Now I knew what she reminded me of. It wasn't a *who*, it was a *what*. She definitely had to be a teacher.

"How did you know where to find me?" I said. But I wasn't sure what I meant. Maybe – start at the beginning, go on to the middle and then get to the finish? She was the kind of person who could do that, no problem.

I started spooning the soup into my mouth.

"Let's just say your kind friend, the Professor, sought me out. All right? Now, finish the lot of it."

The Prof came back with a towel and some clothes and Madame Picard looked the other way while I changed into them. I was nearly warm all the way through now.

"Have you told him?" the Prof asked. She shook her head. "I've only started," she said. "First things first."

She waited until I had finished dressing and was sitting down again.

"Jonas, I teach in the school your sister went to, but I didn't know her because she was much too young for my class. Madame Odile taught her. You know that lady?"

Of course I did. At the beginning of every year Madame Odile had sweets for everyone in her class. Even with the war on she'd managed to get sweets from somewhere. Madame Odile had thought Nadia's stories were great. She'd pinned them on the wall and stuck stars on them.

"When Ulysse, that's my brother-in-law, told me about the round-up that was going to happen on that dreadful day in July, he nearly left it too late. Typical of the man. But I went straight to Madame Odile. There was no point in me fooling around, trying to figure out which girl was Nadia out of all the..." She stopped. "I'll have another coffee, if you don't mind, Professor."

She looked at me exactly as if she knew what I was thinking. But not the way La Giaconda did. The way a teacher did, with eyebrows.

"Madame Odile isn't usually bossy the way I am, but when she is, she's far more terrifying. She gets things done. She got down to the Vél d'Hiv early that morning when the buses started coming in. She stood there, inspecting everybody, and nobody dared say boo to her, because she looks like everybody's granny. Which was the whole point."

She gulped down the coffee. "When she saw Nadia getting out of the bus with your parents, she went right over, lifted her up and kissed her. She told the policemen they'd made a monumental error – that was the phrase she used, she said. To scare them. She told them Nadia was her granddaughter and that your mother sometimes minded her. She told the police not to make fools of themselves. I wish I'd seen her." She shook her head. "I really do. And your sister is cut from the same cloth, by all accounts. She knew exactly what to do."

Nadia had gone with Madame Odile without making any fuss at all. She'd turned round at the street corner and waved to Mama and Papa. Then she'd taken Madame Odile's hand again and they'd walked on, away from the vélodrome, all the way to Madame Odile's apartment in Montparnasse. It was too early for ordinary buses.

"She had a safe place organized for Nadia by the end of the day. She's not in Paris, Jonas, but she's safe and well and she has new papers, just like you. And now I'll be able to let her know that you're safe too. Though I won't say where you are. The Professor tells me you're going somewhere in Normandy."

"But … where *is* Nadia?"

She reached out a hand to brush the damp hair off my face. "Oh, Jonas, even I don't know that. All Madame Odile will tell me is that she's living near the sea. With a nice family. Safe as any child can be these days. But when all this is over…"

She stopped. "If you write a letter to your sister, I'll give it to Madame Odile. That would be the best thing. Just don't write down any names or places. Just tell her you're safe and well and that you have excellent friends."

The Prof nodded. "He can write it tonight and I'll bring it to you. But, Madame Picard, you must go now before it gets dark. Or before the snow freezes over."

She got up, picked up her coat and pulled it around herself. Then she held her hand out to me.

"Write your sister something that only you and she know about, Jonas. Then she'll believe it's really from you, and isn't made up by one of us. That's important. You must stand together now as a family, just the two of you."

She messed my hair up again. Then she was gone.

CORRESPONDENCE

Dear Sister,

I hope you still have d'Artagnan. I began to make an albatross for your theatre but it didn't work out. If you get a chance to make one, they are seabirds with huge wings that used to fly over Paris millions of years ago. You will also need to make a cat like Grimaldi. Then you can put on this play.

THE NEW MUSKETEERS

D'ARTAGNAN: I tried to discover where the princess was hiding. But the Cardinal's men were too many for me.

ALBATROSS: I soared above the city on my great wings. I looked right and left and right again even though there are no traffic lights in the sky. But not even a fairground to lay an egg on did I see.

GRIMALDI: The streets will be very quiet when all the children leave the city. But they will come back, with many fishes for me, the Cat Who Fishes. All the way from the seaside and the big river.

D'ARTAGNAN: The princess and I will triumph in the end and the Cardinal will lose much more than his foot this time.

ALBATROSS: The princess will also get a hat of ostrich feathers, which I will pluck from those crazy birds and bring to her all the way from Africa.

GRIMALDI: And I will eat the rest of the ostrich all by myself. Hey Diddle Diddle, the Cat and the Harp!

It's not much of a play but I didn't have time to do better. You can add anything you like to it, or change it.

I hope you are well. I'm learning lots of music and I'm sure you're learning new things too. We'll have lots to talk about when we see ech other again.

I'm sending you this 50 francs for your ninth birthday

even though that isn't until March. Read what's written on it and you'll know it must be true.

    Love from

        Your brother

Dear Professor,

I'm sorry I was so much trouble to you. And for spoiling your good scarf. I didn't tell you last night because I was afraid to, but I also lost your wife's music case. I didn't know it was hers when I took it. I am very sorry.

    I am leaving you the last of my Deyrolle notebooks as a gift for Christmas. I've used up all the others. Will you mind them for me, but please not read them? Everything is in the trunk and so is my will. I wrote that when I came here first, when I was very afraid. I never had the books and the comics and the roller skates here with me anyway, so maybe it's best to forget about the will. I have the money in case I need it and I've brought the flea circus carriages with me, because Papa made them for me. I know Signor Corrado wouldn't mind.

    If you ever meet him, or La Giaconda, or Alfredo again, please give them my love. I hope they are enjoying much success. I hope Tommaso got into Nadia's school.

    I know Mama and Papa would want to thank you from the bottom of their hearts so I will just have to do it for them. Mama was right – you are a great teacher of music.

I never had a grandfather but I'm sure you would be the best kind to have.

I hope you will be able to travel to the United States and meet your son in the end.

Wishing you well, and a happy Christmas too.

Love,

Jonas

SOMEWHERE

I know it isn't safe to bring these notebooks on the train so I won't. The Prof told me the Nazis are always making checks, at all the stations and even on the trains. But I hate leaving them behind because they are a testament to all the Alber family, not just to me.

There won't be a Jonas Alber living in France any more after tomorrow. There hasn't been a Nadia Alber living there either, not since July. I wasn't able to tell Nadia my new name and I don't know hers. But we will both know we are Somewhere.

I didn't find out anything about Mama and Papa. Nobody knows where Léopold Alber and Anne Berlioz Alber are now. Probably the Germans do, because they make lists of everyone, like Papa said. But not even the policeman was able to find anything out. So I don't know if they are somewhere or not. And I *know* what that means.

If I think about that I just feel the cold going right into my bones, even though I'm inside and the snow is outside. Then it's like Mama and Papa are outside too, always, because I don't know where they are. The window is black, just like the windows in the métro, and the snow is always falling on them.

I can only think what they would say if they *did* read this testament, especially today's bit. Then I can almost see their faces turning around to look at me, just for a minute.

Papa would be really pleased at what I did to Pimply Arms today. Mama would be furious I went out at all, especially when Madame Picard came to see us anyway, to tell us about Nadia. I wouldn't tell Mama that I was afraid all the time. I'd just have to say it was really good practice for turning into somebody else.

They'd be sorry to see Jonas Alber disappear, but they'd be glad he has new papers, just like Nadia.

So, Mama and Papa, I promise you Grégoire Volet will do his best. That's all anyone can do.

ADVICE NOTE:

These three notebooks were surrendered in one lot to Deyrolle, 46 rue du Bac, Paris, for safekeeping on 17 January 1945 by Corporal Robert Clavel of the United States 44th Infantry Division.

Please file under Property to Be Claimed.

AFTERWORD

Jonas and Nadia Alber are fictional characters. But many children like them survived what remained of the Occupation of France, which lasted until summer 1944. Many unaccompanied Jewish children were welcomed by other French families. Others survived in schools and orphanages, in both zones of the country, even after German troops invaded the unoccupied zone in November 1942. Some were betrayed.

Sadly, it is most unlikely that the Alber parents would have survived. Of approximately 76,000 Jews who were deported from France to concentration camps, including 13,152 rounded up and held at the Vél d'Hiv in Paris on 16 July 1942, fewer than 2,500 returned.

After the war in France was over, there was a long period of confusion for families who had been split up. Many organizations worked to put returned adults and children back in touch with their families. But for some this took a long time. Jonas and Nadia would have been luckier.

AUTHOR BIOGRAPHY

MARY FINN is a Dubliner. She has worked as a journalist and a parliamentary reporter, trades that may – or may not – have helped her along the way to write three historical novels and one guidebook. Her previous novels are *Anila's Journey* and *The Horse Girl*. (The guidebook is out of print but several predictions in it came true.)

For Mary, the inspiration for *No Stars at the Circus* came during a visit to Paris when she noticed the plaques erected on many school walls throughout the city. Each plaque marks the disappearance of that school's Jewish pupils during the Nazi occupation of Paris during World War II. Mary began to imagine what life might have been like for a boy who disappeared from his school but survived in hiding. Many of the details of life in wartime Paris – including the circus at the heart of the story – were suggested by the photographs of Robert Doisneau.

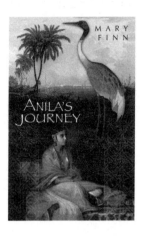

An advert appears in the *Calcutta Gazette*: a scholar
is looking for an apprentice draughtsman to accompany
him on an expedition to record avian life in Bengal.
How can Anila Tandy, left to fend for herself in a city
of rogues, dare to apply for a position that is clearly not
meant for her? But the talented "Bird Girl of Calcutta"
has never shrunk from a challenge. And perhaps
this voyage up the Ganges might be just the thing
to equip Anila in her search for her father, missing
for years and presumed dead.

**"I loved this beautiful story set
in eighteenth-century India, with all its sights,
sounds and smells."** *Jamila Gavin*

18th-century Lincolnshire: Thomas, who is dyslexic, has never met anyone remotely like Ling – wild, carefree, determined – and he falls in love. Ling's horse, Belladonna, has been stolen and Ling fears she is in the hands of the painter Mr George Stubbs, known for flaying horses to learn about their anatomy. When Thomas and Ling pay Stubbs a visit, they learn the true whereabouts of Belladonna, and Thomas is offered a job with Stubbs, who also teaches him to read and write. Thomas and Ling devise a plan to steal back Belladonna, knowing, if caught, Ling could pay with her life.

"Absorbing." *The Irish Times*